Melanie frowned. "You aren't going to give me an inch, are you?"

Vince knew the moment he'd lost the battle, which was the second their gazes met. Her nose wrinkled, making the smattering of freckles dance on her cheeks. He couldn't keep his gaze away from them.

"Well?" she demanded when he didn't answer her.

"Well?" he repeated. "What?"

"I can put the office back the way it was—which, for the record, was completely messy and disorganized, in case you hadn't noticed." The frown that followed her comment wasn't, Vince thought, completely convincing.

"You would, wouldn't you?" From the look in her eye, he thought she just might. That made him smile.

Then again, she might be teasing him, although he couldn't be certain. She was hard to figure out. Whatever else was to be said about Melanie Frazer, she was nothing if not interesting.

And determined.

And absolutely beautiful.

Books by Deb Kastner

Love Inspired

A Holiday Prayer
Daddy's Home
Black Hills Bride
The Forgiving Heart
A Daddy at Heart
A Perfect Match
The Christmas Groom
Hart's Harbor
Undercover Blessings
The Heart of a Man
A Wedding in Wyoming
His Texas Bride
The Marine's Baby
A Colorado Match

DEB KASTNER

lives and writes in colorful Colorado with the front range of the Rocky Mountains for inspiration. She loves writing for the Steeple Hill Love Inspired line, where she can write about her two favorite things—faith and love. Her characters range from upbeat and humorous to (her favorite) dark and brooding heroes. Her plots fall anywhere in between, from a playful romp to the deeply emotional.

Deb's books have been twice nominated for the *RT Book Reviews* Reviewer's Award for Best Book of the Year for Steeple Hill.

Deb and her husband share their home with their two youngest daughters. Deb is thrilled about the newest member of the family—her first granddaughter, Isabella. What fun to be a granny!

Deb loves to hear from her readers. You can contact her by email at DEBWRTR@aol.com, or on her MySpace or Facebook pages.

A Colorado Match
Deb Kastner

Steeple Hill®

Published by Steeple Hill Books™

STEEPLE HILL BOOKS

Steeple
Hill®

Recycling programs
for this product may
not exist in your area.

ISBN-13: 978-0-373-81536-4

A COLORADO MATCH

Copyright © 2011 by Debra Kastner

www.SteepleHill.com

Printed in U.S.A.

"My son," the father said, "you are always with me, and everything I have is yours."
—*Matthew* 15:31

For Joe

Chapter One

Vincent Morningway leaned heavily on his crutches, attempting—not entirely successfully—to write coherently with one hand, keep the telephone to his ear with the other hand and not completely lose his balance and pitch straight down on his backside. He sighed as he finished his call and dropped the receiver back in the cradle.

Stupid crutches.

Stupid cast.

Stupid skiing accident.

He'd unknowingly skied over a patch of hidden ice and had catapulted into a tree. He supposed he ought to be thankful that his injuries weren't any worse than a broken leg and a slight concussion; but at the moment, he didn't feel very blessed.

The whole incident still frustrated him every time he thought about it—which was every time he tried to move.

Growing up in the Rocky Mountains, he'd been skiing almost as long as he'd been walking. Didn't it just figure that the one day a year he allowed himself some downtime to get away from the lodge and pursue an activity he was passionate about, he had to go and get hurt.

Even without his injury, he was already angry at himself for taking time off at all, what with the recent fire that had laid waste to the day care on Morningway Lodge property. Pop and Nate, Vince's interfering younger brother, had ganged up on him, insisting he not cancel his plans.

So much for heeding Nate's advice, he thought sardonically. Ever since they were children, Nate had always managed to get Vince into trouble, yet another instance of an entire lifetime of strife between him and his brother.

Vince was still frowning when the bell over the front door suddenly rang out. He glanced up, adjusted his rectangular black glasses and pasted a polite smile on his face. No matter how out of sorts he was, he still had a job to do. People depended on him, and no matter how he felt, he would not let them down.

A petite redhead whisked in and delicately stamped her feet on the mat just inside the front door, then brushed her free hand down her slim blue skirt. In her other arm she firmly clutched a black leather satchel. She was wearing some kind of spiky high-heeled shoes, which Vince privately thought wasn't the best idea, given that there were several inches of snow on the ground.

What kind of woman made such an obviously foolish judgment call? Either she was brand-new to Colorado, or simply too stubborn to give up her heels for something practical. If he'd had to guess, based on the determined look in her eyes, Vince would have to go with the latter.

"It's freezing outside," she commented as she tossed her mop of unruly, shoulder-length red curls with a tart flip of her chin. She had large, copper-penny eyes and an engaging smile, and she carried such an aura of untapped energy about her in the way she moved that she made him tired just watching her.

After she was satisfied she'd removed all the snow from her shoes, she glided toward the desk, so lightly that it seemed to Vince her feet barely touched the ground, and yet her riotous curls continued to bounce around her shoulders.

"I'm Melanie Frazer."

Her smile widened, if that were possible, showing two perfectly straight, dazzling lines of white teeth. A Garfield grin, Vince thought; a smile that was at once so confident and friendly that it lit up the entire room, but which carried just the slightest hint of mischief. She thrust her hand forward to shake his, and then pursed her lips thoughtfully as her gaze dropped to his crutches.

All at once, she scrunched up her face so that the freckles brushing her nose and cheeks seemed to dance and snatched her hand back before Vince had the chance to move at all, much less make any kind of awkward attempt to shake hands with her, given his crutches.

"Sorry. I didn't realize you…" She let the rest of her sentence drop off as her brow knit even further. "I imagine it's probably difficult for you to shake hands with anybody right now."

It was an obvious statement, but also a thoughtful one, Vince thought. Most people wouldn't have considered how unwieldy his crutches made his movements, especially ones that required the use of his hands.

Or walking, but that was a different matter. He hoped he wouldn't have to embarrass himself by hobbling around where she could see it, given how clumsy he was with the clutches. Whatever the learning curve was on these things, it was too high for Vince.

The woman shrugged, almost as if she'd been reading his thoughts. As quickly as her disconcerted expression had appeared, it was gone in a blink; replaced by the same pretty smile she'd shown him earlier, so honest and genuine that it reached her lustrous eyes.

"Melanie Frazer," she repeated, emphasizing each syllable slightly, as if he were hard of hearing. Her right eyebrow lifted and lowered. She was staring intently at him, clearly expecting…

Something.

He didn't know what she wanted. Or who she was, for that matter, although she clearly thought he should.

He'd already checked the register for guests arriving today, and her name wasn't on it. She could be a passing traveler who mistook the lodge for a bed and breakfast, which happened from time to time, but Vince didn't think so. He had the impression that maybe she was about to attempt to sell him something, although she had offered no more than her name.

"BBS. Boulder Business Services?" she prompted.

Vince shook his head, but Melanie's statement reaffirmed his notion that she was some sort of salesperson. However, she wasn't acting like this was a cold call. She was clearly under the impression that he should know what she was talking about, but he didn't have a clue. As far as he could recall, he had never heard of her company before.

It occurred to him that someone at some other lodge might be waiting for her. In her defense, there were several establishments tucked along the highway, although most of them were closer to Estes Park.

Still, it was a stretch to believe she'd made such an error, given the fact that Morningway Lodge wasn't exactly right off the highway. More like *off-off,* built privately, farther into the woods. And she was acting so completely and utterly sure of herself that Vince wondered if his own judgment was a little off-kilter.

He shook his head again. "I'm sorry. I really don't know who…"

She leveled her gaze at him and cut him off. "The sign outside says Morningway Lodge." She indicated the direction with a tiny jerk of her chin.

"Yes, but—"

"And you are Vincent Morningway."

It wasn't a question, but he nodded anyway.

"Perfect," she said, nodding back at him and placing her hands palms down on the front desk. "Then I'm definitely in the right place."

Vince adjusted his weight on his crutches and leaned back. He had the oddest impression that she was invading his personal space, even though all five feet three inches of her was still standing on the opposite side of the counter. This had to be the most unusual conversation he'd ever had, and it was definitely the most remarkable. To say he was confused would have been an understatement.

The bell rang again, crashing into Vince's thoughts. His gaze automatically flashed toward the front door. His younger brother, Nate, burst through, his face flushed from the cold bite of the outdoor air and his breath heaving as if he'd been running.

"Ms. Frazer," he stated, jogging up to Melanie. "I'm Nate Morningway. And I'm so sorry that I'm late."

The man who approached Melanie was clearly military—or rather, ex-military, as his hair was growing out and he had a day's worth of stubble on his cheeks. He looked years younger than Vince, although the two were clearly related, both with strong, chiseled facial features, firm jaws and similar muscular builds.

Nate reached for her hand and pumped it vigorously.

"Gracie—that's my baby girl—apparently took my car keys off the table when I wasn't looking." He grinned self-deprecatingly. He seemed to be the type of man who relied upon his inherent charm to get him where he needed to go. Not like his brother, Vince, who, even upon their short acquaintance, struck Melanie as somewhat stiff and unyielding.

"I guess I left the keys too close to the edge," Nate continued. "I looked for them, but for all I know, they're in the bottom of Gracie's toy box. Anyway, I finally gave up the search and decided to jog over to meet you. It's only a mile or so."

Melanie chuckled, half at the humorous story Nate was relating, and half in relief that someone actually knew who she was and, by extension—hopefully—why she was here. Vince's bewilderment and the odd way he had reacted when she'd mentioned her name and the company she worked for had thrown her off a little bit.

"I'm the guy who hired you," Nate explained.

"My file says my services are for *Vincent* Morningway," she stated, a little confused.

Her hand tightened on her satchel. She was prepared, as she always was upon embarking on a new project, and she knew she wasn't wrong about this. Vincent Morningway. Morningway Lodge. Built to accommodate families of those recuperating at a nearby physical rehabilitation hospital, she recalled from the research she'd done.

"Yes," Nate agreed easily, and then poked a thumb toward Vince. "That's him. Vince Morningway—my *older* brother," he said in a teasing tone of voice.

"Vince," Nate continued as a formal introduction, "this is Melanie Frazer. She's going to be your new business consultant. She's here to—"

"Excuse me?" Vince interrupted, sounding exasperated. "Give me some frame of reference because I don't know what you're talking about. What did you do this time, Nate?"

At first Melanie thought Vince had taken offense at Nate's off-the-cuff jesting, but upon reflection, she decided it was more than that. Vince's words were no less than an accusation, and sounded strained and harassed. Melanie's gaze immediately switched to his direction.

Vince was glaring daggers at his brother, and the muscle in the corner of his jaw twitched rhythmically, a probable indication that he was genuinely annoyed with Nate.

"What did you do this time?" Vince demanded.

For some reason Vince's change in demeanor struck Melanie as odd and out of character for him. It was a complete turnaround from her initial assessment. He'd appeared fatigued, maybe, but not cross. He'd been perfectly polite with her, and his gaze was kind.

As was her habit—possibly a bad one—she had already formed an opinion about the man she'd be working with. She'd had too much personality profiling training, she supposed.

The first thing she'd noticed when she'd entered the lodge was how endearingly disheveled Vince looked. Although his smile was strained at the corners, his bright blue eyes were clear and friendly. His sports coat was several years out of style, and his hair looked like he'd combed it with a firecracker.

Dark brown hair tumbled over his brow, and Melanie noted the single streak of silver coursing through it, a telltale sign as to how stressed and overworked the man really was; that, and the lines of fatigue that marred his brow, only slightly concealed by his rectangular black-rimmed glasses, probably the only contemporary piece of his entire wardrobe.

Still, he was a good-looking guy, all things being equal. And if nothing else, his currently tousled appearance was a clear indication of how useful her services could be for him—or rather, for Morningway Lodge.

"I can help you," she assured him.

Obviously his younger brother thought as much, or he would never have hired her. Vince simply didn't yet comprehend what her business could do for *his* business. In her experience, a few simple changes in one's business practices could translate to a substantial savings in both time and money—the investors', the *family's* bottom line.

On BBS's intake form for Morningway Lodge, presumably filled out by his brother, she'd discovered that Vince didn't use a computer—for *anything*. Not even his financials. Given that information, she guessed he probably didn't even know what a smartphone was, never mind how to use it to improve his business practices. Talk about the dark ages.

"This is going to be good for you," Nate insisted, and Melanie had to agree.

Melanie was about to spread some serious light into Vince's world, like the sunshine breaking through the clouds after a storm. All it would take her was six short weeks and a little cooperation from Vince.

Mentally, she ticked off the most crucial items, knowing she would make copious to-do lists as soon as she'd taken a real look around, her being a perfectionist and all. She would organize his workspace and streamline his paperwork, mostly onto computer spreadsheets, saving him an enormous amount of time in the long run. She would show him how to enter his financials on a computer, giving him greater accuracy as well as saving him time. If she thought it would help him, she'd introduce him to a smartphone, or at least a digital organizer.

"I'm not inclined to anger," Vince said, his brow furrowed. He wasn't going to make this easy for her, but tough cases were her specialty.

She sighed inwardly. She suspected Nate had sprung this idea on Vince with no forewarning, and she couldn't blame him for his annoyance and confusion.

That being said, she could do without the extra hassle of trying to justify what she was here to do for him, or else face the serious possibility of losing this account entirely—*not* a good way to get a promotion in her company.

Patience wasn't exactly one of her virtues. She wasn't the type to sit still and wait, especially with a very attractive promotion—which she'd worked hard for—just one project away. This one last assignment and then she'd have the luxury of a cushy desk job. The director of operations position was hers.

It was so close she could taste it.

If she fixed the problems at Morningway Lodge.

She had the sneaking suspicion that Vince Morningway wasn't going to make it easy on her.

Chapter Two

Vince was livid. Nate was grinning as smugly as the proverbial cat that had eaten an entire *cage* of canaries, and Melanie was staring at Vince as if he were her next challenging project.

Which he wasn't. He was already shaking his head to the contrary.

"Just hear her out," Nate appealed earnestly, which only served to make Vince even more stiff-necked about whatever was going on. If it was Nate's idea, it was a bad one. He didn't need Melanie to explain *that* to him.

"Boulder Business Services," Melanie said, jumping in on the tail of Nate's comment, "offers consulting services to businesses ranging from small family-owned operations, to large corporate entities. I can assure you we're the best firm in the business, and of course I can offer you a list of references if you'd like."

Not necessary.

He didn't need references because she wouldn't be working here. He was convinced this was just another one of Nate's shenanigans meant to get on Vince's nerves, and it wasn't going to work. Not this time.

For Melanie's sake, he would be polite, but only until he figured out a way to turn her down without hurting her feelings. She seemed to be a nice enough woman, and it infuriated him that Nate would put her in the middle of their feud without regard to her point of view.

"Consulting?" he asked aloud, stalling for time while he thought of a solution to this problem.

"From what I've read in my file, you are a bit behind the times in some of your business practices," she explained, her voice gaining momentum as she got into her subject, about which she was clearly enthusiastic. "First we'll deal with the smaller organizational issues within your office, like your desk and filing system. Then I'll help you streamline the majority of your work onto your computer, which will do wonders in regard to running your office more efficiently."

She smiled confidently, first at Vince, then Nate, then back to Vince again. "I'm here to bring your business into the twenty-first century."

Surely she must be aware that she sounded like a television infomercial. He wasn't buying any of it; but if he was, her charming, toothy grin would be mighty persuasive.

What did that even mean, bringing his business into the twenty-first century? Did he really look that out of touch to her? Some hermit hiding in the woods?

And what was up with Nate, springing this woman and her *consulting* business on him and then waiting for him to work out the details?

Vince narrowed his gaze on Nate for a moment before he turned a polite smile on Melanie. "I appreciate your offer, but I don't need any help. I run the business just fine on my own, thank you."

"*All* on your own," Nate qualified.

Vince didn't say anything because family business was *family* business, but he thought the pointed, eyebrow-arching, And-why-would-that-be? look he gave Nate would be enough to put him in his place.

After all, it was Nate who'd irresponsibly ran off after high school, joined the Marines and left Vince alone to run the lodge by himself. He'd been left to cope with everything alone, and it was because of Nate.

Nate visibly winced and smiled sheepishly, and then nodded, silently acknowledging his faults. At least he had the good grace to realize how ironic his statement had been. Even so, as much as Nate might be helping out around the lodge recently—now that he'd supposedly returned home for good—Vince didn't think it would last. Not with Nate. He couldn't trust his brother as far as he could throw him—although he *could* still throw him.

"You won't let Pop and me hire you a personal assistant," Nate explained.

"Because we can't afford it," Vince said, becoming weary of this whole conversation, and wishing Melanie wasn't present to hear any of it. He wasn't the kind of man to air his dirty laundry publicly, be it family or business; and he found it rather humiliating that Nate heedlessly seemed determined to do just that.

"What would be the point? Why should I hire someone to do what I can do all by myself?"

"Says you," countered Nate. "How long do you think you can keep up this pace all by yourself?"

Vince leveled a look on him. "As long as I have to."

"You're running yourself ragged," Nate insisted, adamantly shaking his head.

"I have to agree with Nate," Melanie chimed in.

Of course she did. Everyone always agreed with Nate. But this was none of her business, and Vince wanted to keep it that way.

"Look," he said, making an awkward placating gesture that was cut short by his crutches, "No offense, Melanie, but your services really aren't needed. I'm sorry you came all this way for nothing."

Melanie leaned as far over the counter as her short frame would allow.

"I think Nate is right," she repeated, as if Vince hadn't heard her the first time around. "I really think I can help you."

What was with everyone? He was being none-too-gently coerced into a corner and he knew it. They had his arm behind his back, figuratively speaking, and now they were starting to twist it tight.

Nate, Pop and now Melanie. He couldn't argue with everyone.

But he had to try. And he knew just how to do it.

"We don't have the money." The lack of working capital was the basis for his original argument, and he decided he would stick with it.

Melanie wasn't going to work for free.

"This is a ministry, not a multimillion-dollar corporation. The families of patients rehabilitating at the RMPR Hospital have enough to deal with without the burden of having to stay at an overpriced hotel."

He saw the corners of Melanie's lips turn down just slightly, and only for a second, but he knew he'd said something she didn't want to hear. Probably that she wasn't going to get paid.

"Good grief," Melanie muttered under her breath. Or at least that was how it sounded to Vince.

"Sorry, bro," Nate said with a laugh. "We've already thought of that—the money part of it, I mean. That's why you're getting a business consultant and not a personal assistant. This is a one-time thing, and I'm footing the bill for it out of my own savings."

Vince wasn't happy, and he wasn't the least bit convinced about any of this, but with each passing second, it was becoming more difficult to find a way out of the predicament.

He sighed. "One day? One week? What?"

"One *time*," Melanie corrected. "The entire process should take about *six* weeks, give or take."

"Don't be so hardheaded," Nate said. "Will you just for once take something that someone is giving you and not put up such a fuss about it?"

Melanie gave a clipped little nod. Vince thought she might be agreeing with Nate.

Again.

"I don't have the time," he argued. "As you pointed out, my leg is in a cast. It's going to take me longer to do things, even without having Melanie...here," he finished lamely. He had been going to say *underfoot,* but that seemed a little too blunt, even for him.

"Make time," Nate countered.

"And if I say no?" Vince knew it sounded like a taunt, and he was immediately convinced he shouldn't have asked the question at all. Nate was gloating.

"I'll force you. I've already paid the bill up front. You wouldn't stiff me like that, would you?" Nate offered up his most placating smile.

Vince lifted an eyebrow and then shrugged. "You're sure about that?"

"Maybe not, if it was just me," Nate replied with a wicked smile. "But Pop agrees with *me* on this one. Give it up, bro. You'd better get used to the idea because you are officially out of options."

Vince wanted to kick something, except that his leg was already in a cast and Melanie was still looking on. He could argue with Nate all day and night if he had to, but there was no way he would argue with his father.

The man was still in a wheelchair from a recent stroke, which was why Vince was doing all the work in the first place. Pop's condition seemed to be improving now that Nate was home and had presented him with a granddaughter, but Vince didn't want to take any chances with his father's health.

Melanie cleared her throat and smiled, reminding the men of her presence.

Vince wanted to cringe. She'd been standing there the entire time, absorbing all this personal information about the two brothers without saying a single thing. How completely and utterly mortifying.

But she spoke now. "I promise I'll make the process as painless as possible for you."

"It's for your own good," Nate prodded.

Vince couldn't stand Nate being the victor of this game, but neither could he see a way out of this predicament except by going through with it. And it was just like his brother to rub it in.

Vince had the uncomfortable inkling, like a wisp of cool air creeping up the back of his neck, that working with Melanie was going to be anything but painless. He sighed and, leaning heavily on his left crutch, pushed his glasses up his nose and scrubbed his fingers through his hair with his right hand.

His head hurt. His leg hurt.

And he'd officially been had.

Vince groaned and pulled up a three-legged stool, seating himself gingerly and leaning his elbows on the front counter at the main lodge. He wanted to cocoon himself in the back office, but there was no one at present to watch the desk. His leg was throbbing and itching and driving him crazy—but not as much as the woman determined to *make his life easier.*

He didn't know how he was going to get any work done. He'd never been so distracted in his life. He sat for a good ten minutes staring at the same piece of paper and then realized he hadn't yet read a word of it.

He kept thinking about Melanie. And it wasn't just about the enormous disturbance she was going to create in his admittedly clutter-filled life over the next few weeks.

Every time he closed his eyes, he saw a brilliant copper-eyed gaze, red curls and a freckled nose. Even the cute little quirk of her right eyebrow came to mind, and he didn't know why.

Melanie Frazer was going to be nothing but trouble.

Worse yet, Nate had offered her a room at the lodge so she wouldn't have to commute from Boulder. With Vince's luck, she'd be tailing him everywhere, at all hours of the day. At the very least, he knew she was foaming at the mouth to get started *organizing* him. His shoulders tensed just thinking about it. He was a private person. His stuff was *his stuff.*

Scowling, he reached for the next stack of papers and stared unseeingly at the one on top. The bell over the front door rang, and he pulled in a breath and held it as he looked up, knowing it was going to be Melanie. Both a smile and a frown wrestled in his expression.

"I thought you might be hiding," she teased as she brushed curls from her eyes with the palm of her hand. At least she had dressed more sensibly today, in khaki pants and a chocolate-brown sweater that complemented her eyes.

More to the point, she was wearing a pair of hiking boots—new ones, he judged thoughtfully. They'd probably give her a blister or two as she broke them in, but they were still better than high heels by a mile.

"What would be the point?" Vince's smile was winning the war against the frown, despite his annoyance at Nate for getting him into this situation in the first place.

"Mmm," she agreed, cocking her head to one side as she studied him. "Sensible man."

Vince cringed inwardly, although he was careful not to let it show on his face. She was teasing him, of course, but the words hit home nonetheless.

A sensible man. He'd been called that before.

It was practically his call sign. If he were charming and witty like his brother, he'd know how to handle a woman like Melanie, instead of tripping over his tongue—and his thoughts, for that matter—all the time.

Hogwash.

He didn't want to be like Nate. He had enough to think about just being himself. He had a job to do, as did Melanie. And her job, the way he understood it, was to make a nuisance of herself. The sooner she realized he wasn't the type of man to change things around on a whim, the better off they all would be.

It was as simple as that. Or not.

He reached for his crutches and hobbled to the door separating the front office from the main room. Melanie scrambled forward to help him hold the door, and then hovered near his elbow as he awkwardly hopped toward the furniture surrounding the central fireplace.

He didn't know what she expected to be able to do if he lost his balance. A tiny little thing like her couldn't possibly catch him from falling.

"The doctor says I have to keep this cast on for six weeks," he said, trying for a conversational tone as he dropped to a seat on the sofa.

"It's bright red," she remarked, staring at his fluorescent cast.

"Yeah," he agreed with a chuckle, thinking more of the color of her hair than of his cast. "They have all kinds of nifty colors to choose from these days."

"Does it hurt?" She took a seat next to him on the couch and crossed her feet at the ankles.

"It itches. I'll live. Six weeks, if I'm on good behavior."

"I beg your pardon?"

"The cast. I'll get it off in six weeks."

"Oh," she said, sounding relieved. "For a moment there I thought you were talking about me."

Vince shook his head. He was thinking about her, but he wasn't talking about her.

"Good, because you're not getting rid of me."

She was almost as blunt and straight-to-the-point as he was, and it took him aback. He stared at her for a long moment, wondering if there was anything he could say to dissuade her from her purpose.

From the look on her face, *not much*. Unless,

of course, he could convince her she was wasting her time.

Which shouldn't be that hard to do, all things being equal. His daily life was anything but glamorous; and really, having a cast on his leg wasn't any huge hindrance to the mountains of paperwork on his desk that he had to tackle this afternoon. How exciting was that? She'd soon find that there was little she could do to remove the mind-numbing pace of running the lodge, and his business system, while not as up-to-date as she'd no doubt like to see it, worked for him.

More or less.

Maybe she would see he was hopeless and just leave him alone.

His work—his *life*—could be summed up in three words: boring, tedious and dull. Okay, and maybe unsystematic, but certainly not chaotic.

For the tiniest moment he wished he had something exciting going on in his life, something that would spark the interest of a beautiful, successful woman like Melanie.

Yeah, right. Like that would ever happen. Besides, it was the lodge she was interested in—not him personally. He scoffed internally at his own foolish musings.

Better she learned the truth up front. And better he keep his mind where it belonged—on the lodge.

And *not* on a certain redhead.

Chapter Three

It was hard for Melanie to concentrate with Vince's clear, blue-eyed gaze on hers. He was probably wondering what kind of valid help she could possibly be to him.

If he knew the truth, he'd be bolting out the door without looking back.

She was about to rock his life—or the business part of it, anyway. The thought made her smile inwardly, although she kept her expression carefully neutral as Vince sized her up as if she were some kind of competition to him, like players on the opposing sides of a field.

He really didn't get that they were supposed to be teammates here. She was working *for* him, not against him, but she sensed it would take her a while to get that piece of information through his thick skull. He had been perfectly polite, of course, but she knew he didn't want her there. No doubt he was thinking of the quickest and most efficient way to get rid of her.

Which wasn't going to happen.

Nevertheless, she was relieved when he finally looked away. It disconcerted her to have him staring at her so intently, especially when he cocked his head and flashed her a secretive smile.

"So…" he began, and then let his sentence dangle uncomfortably.

"So?" she challenged. She tipped her chin up and met his reflective gaze again, ignoring how ill at ease it made her feel to do so.

"What am I supposed to do with you?" he mused aloud, tapping a finger on his chin, right over the charming dimple that divided his strong, square jaw.

"Simple. Let me help you. This process is going to go a lot easier for both of us if you step back and allow me to do my work."

He stared at her a moment more before speaking. The expression on his face didn't change, but the sudden spark in his eyes let her know something was afoot.

"Okay," he said at last.

"Okay?" she repeated, completely in shock. After the scene yesterday, she hadn't really expected him to give in so easily. Or give in at *all,* really. He'd seemed too stubborn to go down without a fight. And now he was conceding?

"Sure." His gaze narrowed as he smiled, or smirked, more like. Something was definitely afoot in Vince's mind, and Melanie knew she wasn't going to like whatever it was. "I have some paperwork to do in the back office. Because I'm short on help today, you can cover the front desk for me."

"What?" she said, tempering her voice so it didn't become tight and shrill.

The man was thoroughly exasperating. His eyes retained that amused spark, and the left corner of his lip completely betrayed him when it twitched upward oh so slightly. He was acting remarkably smug.

Did he think he'd won this round?

Well, then, he'd better just think again. She knew what he was up to. She arched her brow, her mind racing. Due to the restrictions laid on him by his family, he couldn't turn her away outright.

But if she quit on her own? That would be an entirely different proposition now, wouldn't it?

He was trying to annoy her on purpose—which would only work if she reacted as he expected her to do. It was, she realized, going to be a remarkably simple thing to turn the tables on him.

"All right, I'll do it," she said, smothering a smile. He wanted to play? She was all in.

He stared at her, looking unconvinced. His smug little smirk turned into a cute little frown, furrowing his brow under the top rim of his glasses.

"Really," she assured him as she stood and walked to the door to the front office. She opened it, gesturing for him to enter before her. "I'm guessing the front desk could use some of my organizational finesse. It's as good a place to start as anywhere. Once you see my work, I know you'll change your mind about me."

Vince shook his head and then nodded, looking a little bit dazed. Then, without a word, he pulled himself to his feet with his crutches and hobbled past her. He looked back only when he'd reached his office door.

"I'm warning you. You're going to get bored.

Fast. There's really nothing to this job but waiting on the guests if they have questions or need extra towels. This time of day it's usually deathly quiet around here."

"I'm glad to hear it," she answered. "Quiet is good. It will give you the chance to sit down and rest that leg of yours, and for me to get some work done."

Vince frowned. "This isn't going to matter, you know. It's only a matter of time before you realize your efforts are futile."

"Let me be the judge of that," she said, twirling her finger to indicate he should turn back toward his office. "Now. You. Go. Sit."

Vince couldn't argue with Melanie. He didn't really *want* to argue with her, when it clearly wasn't going to make a bit of difference. He sat down in his comfortable black leather office chair, resting his head back and pressing over his eyes with his palms. He was getting a tremendous headache, but as he had told Melanie, he had a lot of paperwork to do. With a tired sigh, he leaned forward, opened a ledger and then, for a good ten minutes, rhythmically tapped a pencil against the smooth oak of his desktop.

At this rate he would accomplish nothing. She was already disrupting his routine, and she really hadn't even started meddling yet. How was it going to be when she was standing over his shoulder, analyzing his business practices and criticizing his every move?

He closed his eyes, willing himself to concentrate on the paperwork in front of him. If he could just center his thoughts, he might be able to get something constructive finished; but that wasn't likely to happen, especially because he could hear Melanie bustling about the front desk.

He couldn't imagine what she was finding to do that was making so much noise. He couldn't stand it any longer. Using his desk for leverage, he propped himself up and shuffled out to the front office. He didn't think he'd ever get used to walking with the crutches, and he knew he must look ridiculously awkward and inept.

Heat rushed to his face, and he frowned. He wasn't usually so self-conscious. It wasn't like him at all. These new, confusing feelings had arrived along with Melanie, and he wasn't sure what to do with them.

Melanie whirled about when she heard him,

and for just the slightest moment, her breath-taking copper-colored eyes were wide and blinking, as if he'd caught her in some kind of mischief. It was enough to cause him to hesitate momentarily.

But the startled look was gone, replaced by the self-possessed demeanor he'd already started associating with her personality. Maybe he was imagining things.

"Ta-da!" she announced, sweeping her hand to indicate the front desk area.

"Wow," Vince said, giving a low whistle as his gaze swept across the newly cleaned and organized desk. Every scrap of paper was neatly stacked, the date books were perfectly arranged and opened on the counter and the whole room smelled like some kind of lemon-scented furniture polish.

He hadn't realized how messy he'd let the outer office become until he saw how much of a difference Melanie had made with it. Had the guests seen the same thing? Was he truly that disorganized?

Melanie reached for a tin that held a dozen pencils and pulled them out for his inspection. "See? I even sharpened the pencils for you."

"You really didn't need to do that," he said gruffly, shaking his head.

"Yes, I did," she countered. "I know this project wasn't your idea, and I know you don't want me here. Frankly, that knowledge doesn't exactly make me want to jump for joy at being here either. But if you think you're going to somehow coerce me into quitting, think again. I've got a major promotion riding on this assignment, and I'm not about to lose it because the two of us can't work together. You'd better get used to me being around because I'm here for the duration."

"Are you sure?" he prodded.

She frowned and propped her hands on her hips. "You aren't going to give me an inch, are you?"

He wasn't. Or at least he thought he wasn't.

He knew the moment he'd lost the battle, which was the second their gazes met. Her nose wrinkled, making the smattering of freckles dance on her cheeks. He couldn't keep his gaze away from them.

"Well?" she demanded when he didn't immediately answer her. She sounded a little put out. Probably because he really wasn't paying attention to what she was saying.

Those freckles…

"Well?" he repeated, feeling as lame as he knew he sounded. "What?"

"I can put the office back the way it was—which, for the record, was completely messy and disorganized, in case you hadn't noticed. Everything I've done can be undone except for the pencils."

Her right eyebrow twitched upward. "That is, unless you want me to break all the leads off them, which, at the moment, I'd be happy to do." The frown that followed her comment wasn't, Vince thought, completely convincing. It was more mischievous than anything.

"You would, wouldn't you?" From the look in her eye, he thought she might.

Then again, she might simply be teasing him. He wasn't certain of anything anymore, especially where Melanie was concerned. What he knew about women could fit on the tip of one of those pencils she had sharpened.

Whatever else was to be said about Melanie Frazer, she was nothing if not interesting.

And determined.

And absolutely beautiful.

What could possibly go wrong?

* * *

On her second day officially on the job, she was up and about early. The front desk was vacant; but then again, Melanie thought, it wasn't yet eight o'clock in the morning.

Vince might not even be at his desk yet, although she suspected he would be. Despite their short acquaintance, she'd made abundant notes on the man, particularly in light of her revealing encounter with him the day before. He struck her as a bit of a workaholic.

And he was definitely set in his ways. Like solid concrete.

She eyed the bell on the front counter, and then decided she would simply let herself into the back and check Vince's office to see if he was there. He probably wouldn't be expecting her so early, and for some strange reason it gave her a bit of a rush to think that she might actually catch him off guard.

"Knock, knock," she called as she simultaneously rapped twice on the half-closed door to Vince's office. "Hello? Anybody here?"

She pushed the door open and stuck her head inside the office. Vince was sitting behind his desk, facing her. His expression was harrowed as he stared determinedly at the mountain of receipts towering on his desk. An ink-marked ledger was spread in front of him, and the fingers of his right hand were splayed across the numbers of an ancient-looking adding machine, which was spewing out mounds of ticker tape with an old-fashioned clickety-clack.

He looked up as if in a daze, that same stubborn lock of silver-streaked brown hair tumbling forward and his glasses slightly askew on his nose. He would be an attractive man, she thought, if he wasn't being so difficult about everything.

It would be nice if he smiled once in a while. But of course, the moment their eyes met, his brow knit in consternation. It didn't take a genius to realize he didn't like her. Or at least, he didn't like what she stood for.

Change.

"There was no one at the desk, so I just let myself in. I hope that's okay," she explained in her best business tone. She wasn't going to let his crotchety manner get her down. She wanted to get an early start.

"Already," he groaned. It wasn't a question. He sounded annoyed. So much for second chances.

Too bad for him.

He obviously didn't like it, not even after having been able to sleep on it. He clearly wasn't in a better mood this morning, and she wasn't doing backflips herself, but she had a job to do and a promotion to acquire. Today she was determined to get started—really started—with her work.

Because the sooner she started, the sooner she'd be finished—and she could get away from Vince, this rustic lodge and these horribly uncomfortable hiking boots, which she was wearing due to Vince's questionable advice.

Just let him try to stand in her way.

She was prepared for him. She already knew what the first item on her agenda would be.

Gesturing toward the mountain of receipts in front of him on the desk, she asked, "So what are you doing?"

Vince rubbed the tips of his fingers against his temples and tightened his gaze on her. She knew he was deciding how much information to give her—or even if he wanted to answer the question at all.

After a moment, he dropped his hands back onto the desk and sighed. "I'm preparing the P&L and balance sheet for last month. I'll admit it's not my favorite part of this job, but it has to be done."

"You're working by *hand?*"

"Well, I'm not adding the numbers in my head, if that's what you mean," he said, tapping his fingers on the adding machine.

Melanie's eyebrow arched as she pointed over his right shoulder to a closed laptop computer sitting on the pinewood credenza behind him.

"Have you ever heard of a computer?" she asked, trying to keep the edge from her voice. He really *was* behind the times. She wondered if he knew how much.

He shrugged. "The way I've got it figured, by the time I input all these receipts into the computer, I may as well have done it by hand."

"That's backward thinking," she informed him. "Let me set you up with some computer spreadsheets. You'd be surprised at how much time they save you."

"Not interested," he snapped, gathering stacks of receipts and stuffing them in a manila envelope marked and dated for the previous month with a red felt-tipped pen.

Melanie wouldn't be swayed. "It looks like

your filing system could do with an overhaul as well."

"Do tell." He deliberately turned his back on her as he stuffed the manila envelope into a beat-up metal filing cabinet.

"Look, I know you don't believe me, but give me the benefit of the doubt." Give me a *break,* she thought, although she didn't say it aloud.

Vince glanced at his watch. "How long is this going to take?"

He asked the question as if he expected her to simply file a single folder and be on her way, but she saw the telltale gleam in his eye. He was being intentionally difficult, and they both knew it.

"Weeks, Vince," she said, suddenly tired. "This changeover is going to take *weeks.* Especially with the condition of your office," she added, not realizing until the words were out of her mouth that the remark sounded like a personal jab, when she was really only stating the facts.

"I was planning to start my work today," she continued hurriedly, trying to mask over her previous statement. "Right now, in fact. Unless that's inconvenient for you."

Chapter Four

She belatedly realized she shouldn't have added that last part of the statement because he was going to grasp at any excuse he could to block her directive. With her response, she'd just unintentionally handed one right to him.

She was really going to have to watch her mouth around him, that was for sure. He was an intelligent and quick-witted man. He knew how to take it as well as he gave it. She definitely needed to be on her guard with this guy.

"As a matter of fact," Vince jumped in, without missing a beat, "Jessica should be here any moment, so I'm afraid we simply won't have time just now to start on your *project*." He emphasized the last word just enough to make her want to grind her teeth.

"Jessica?" she queried, wondering if she was somehow supposed to recognize that name, and then deciding he was purposefully baiting her.

"Jessica is Nate's fiancée," he explained, his voice lowering and becoming a bit more gravelly.

His gaze deflected for the tiniest moment, and his lips twitched and one corner pinched together. She had the distinct feeling there was something going on behind the scenes in Vince's mind, and she wondered what it was.

Probably how much he disliked what she was trying to do here. Or maybe how much he disliked what she stood for. Or, possibly the most likely scenario of all, how much he disliked her in general.

As if on cue, a pretty blond-haired woman with a wiggling baby bundled in her arms came sweeping in the door of Vince's office. If she was surprised to see that Vince was not alone, she didn't show it. She flashed Melanie a shy but genuinely friendly smile and turned her gaze toward Vince.

"I hope it's okay that I brought Gracie along," Jessica said, propping the baby in an empty chair to remove her snowsuit. "Nate had to go to Denver for a couple of days to get some supplies for the lodge."

Vince's brow creased for just a moment, but once his gaze alighted on the baby, he was all smiles.

As soon as baby Gracie was free of the restrictive clothing, she wiggled around onto her tummy and scooted off the edge of the chair, kicking her legs as she dangled. Melanie didn't know if she'd ever seen a more adorable baby than the curly-haired little girl; especially when Gracie reached the floor, propped herself into a standing position using the chair for balance, and gave her Uncle Vince a full, cheeky eight-toothed grin.

Vince chuckled and came around the desk, giving the baby a big, smacking kiss on the cheek. "You know I'm always happy to have Gracie here."

He turned to Melanie. "Nate is adopting Gracie, so she's my niece."

The woman smiled at Melanie. "I'm Jessica Sabin, by the way. I'm the day care director here at Morningway Lodge. Or at least, I was. In the interim, I'm working behind the front desk."

She paused and gave Vince an encouraging

smile. "But I'm sure that won't be for long. The ministry the Morningways do here for the families of patients staying at the RMPR Hospital can't be replaced, but buildings sure can be. God will bless us."

"He will," Vince agreed.

Melanie was keenly aware of her sudden, involuntary intake of breath, and she tensed, hoping the other two hadn't heard it. She'd already heard Vince refer to Morningway Lodge as a ministry, so she supposed she should have been prepared for it, but *God talk,* as she thought of it, made her incredibly uncomfortable, bringing to mind other times and other situations she would rather not dwell upon.

"And," Vince continued, thankfully not appearing to notice the change in Melanie's demeanor or breathing pattern, "Jessica forgot to mention she's the local heroine around here. She rescued several children, and even Gracie here, from the fire at the day care center. There would be a lot of grieving parents, my brother included, if it were not for her brave efforts."

Melanie studied the woman with renewed interest. Her gaze had dropped to her feet and she was shifting uncomfortably from foot to foot. Jessica might be a local celebrity, but if the bright pink stain on her cheeks was anything to go by, Melanie thought the poor woman must not care much for the spotlight Vince was beaming her direction.

"I'm Melanie Frazer," she said, knowing how uncomfortable she felt when Vince put *her* on the spot, and wanting to give Jessica a way out of it. "My life story is not nearly as glamorous as yours, but I'm glad to meet you. I'll be staying at the lodge for about six weeks, so I'm sure we'll be seeing each other around."

"Oh?" Jessica asked. "I assumed you were a new employee, since you're in the back office and all."

Vince barked out a dry laugh. "Hardly. Melanie is the *business consultant* Nate hired for me."

When Vince turned away, Jessica rolled her eyes at Melanie in silent woman-to-woman communication. Clearly she was aware of the animosity between the two brothers, but to Melanie's surprise, Jessica didn't try to defend Nate or push the tender subject with Vince.

"You said Nate took off again?" Vince asked with a huff, addressing Jessica, though his back was still turned on her. He whirled around, using one of his crutches to center himself and the other to keep from toppling over.

"Yes, he did. Why?" Jessica smiled patiently. She was being a lot more tolerant with Vince's attitude than Melanie would have been, given the same circumstances.

He pushed his glasses up his nose and scoffed. "It figures."

What was wrong with the man? Melanie thought. Something was certainly stuck in his craw and was eating him away. His Jekyll-and-Hyde disposition was unlike anything Melanie had ever run across in all her years on the job. What was underneath all that bluster?

Maybe that was exactly the question she needed to be asking. As far as her business services went, Melanie found it was helpful to get to know the person she was working for—although to be fair, that was not *exactly* applicable in this case, because Nate had hired her, and not Vince.

And Vince and Nate did not get along. That much was patently clear.

It was no wonder she and Vince had gotten off on the wrong foot, what with Nate bringing her in behind Vince's back and without his knowledge.

But she thought it might be partially her fault things had gone downhill from there. Maybe she'd pushed him too fast in her hunger to get the job done. Maybe if she'd given him a bit more time to get used to the idea, they wouldn't be butting heads so ferociously.

She couldn't help but think maybe she could still turn things around for them and make their working relationship less contentious. *If* she could figure out a way to bridge the gap; and that was a big *if.*

"I was planning to visit the burn site tomorrow morning to see how the cleanup is going," Vince told Jessica. "The youth group from the church is going to help, so I wanted to stop by and thank them. But I guess that won't be happening because I won't have Nate's help. I can't drive my truck with this stupid cast on. It's a standard transmission."

Melanie couldn't have asked for a better opportunity—time with Vince, out of the office, visiting the grounds of a family business that was clearly important to him—even if he did resent the thought of change.

She cleared her throat to remind both Vince and Jessica that she was present, if not exactly part of the conversation.

"No problem. I'll drive you."

* * *

By mid-morning the next day, Vince and Melanie were on their way to the burn site. "The clutch is a bit sensitive," Vince commented as the gears made a slight grinding sound when Melanie shifted from first to second gear. He gave her a sidelong glance out of the corner of his eye.

Her gaze was firmly on the road as she maneuvered the truck up a steep incline. From the way her forehead was creased and her lips were pursed, she was obviously concentrating ferociously.

That, or she was upset about something. It didn't matter either way. Even with her face all scrunched up, she was one pretty lady. He couldn't help but admire her from his peripheral vision.

As they crowned the hill and the blackened remains of the day care came into view, Vince's focus immediately changed. His breath stung in his throat and he swallowed it back. He'd never get used to looking at the razed, utterly desolate land. He imagined it was a bleak sight even for Melanie, who had no vested interest in the place.

Even with the area teeming with life in the

form of teenagers with garbage bags doing what they could to clean up the site, it was still heartbreaking to see. And while he appreciated all the help the youth groups from combined churches in the area were giving him, it was only a scratch on the surface of what needed to be done.

Vince closed his eyes. God was with him, and God was good, he reminded himself. No matter how stark the reality of the situation looked from a human perspective, God was in control. Vince had to believe that.

He *did* believe that.

It was a necessary reminder, and an internal conversation Vince used with himself on a regular basis, especially since the crisis with the day care.

Melanie hit a rut that bounced Vince out of his seat. He automatically reached for the bar over the door and braced himself, although the road wasn't any worse than the usual winter washboard.

"Oh, dear," Melanie said softly, as she cruised the rest of the way down the hill and parked the truck not far from the burn site. "I'm hurting your leg with my bad driving, aren't I?"

Vince opened his eyes and turned his gaze toward her. She was staring back at him with wide, blinking copper-penny eyes and concern lining her face.

"Not at all. I've lived in the mountains all my life. A little washboard can't hurt me." Surprisingly, the smile he flashed her didn't feel forced, even though his spirit had plummeted the moment they'd driven up to the site.

"Well, I'm sorry, just the same."

"Don't be," he said softly.

"Who are all these teenagers?" she asked, clearly eager to change the subject.

"They are a combined youth group from some of the local churches. When they heard about the fire, they offered to help clean the debris."

"For free?"

Despite his melancholy, he smiled. "That's what Christians do. Support each other in times of need."

She snorted. "Not in my experience."

His eyebrows raised in surprise at the vehemence of her denial. "No?"

She shook her head fiercely but didn't offer any details. He was reluctant to push her if she didn't want to talk about it, but he was wondered what kind of *Christians* she'd been around to cause her to feel so much animosity.

"Jessica seems nice," she commented, clearly eager to change the subject.

His smile faltered as a dark cloud briefly passed over his heart.

"What?" she asked. He wondered if that was concern and empathy on her face, or merely curiosity.

"Nothing. It's nothing." He shook his head. He was not the kind of guy who liked to *talk about it*.

"You won't tell me what you were thinking just now?" She was pushing him, but the words were spoken gently and with respect, and Vince suddenly found himself opening up, which was a revelation in itself.

"I was thinking about my mother," he admitted hesitantly.

"Oh? Does she live here at the lodge?"

"She died when I was a teenager."

"I'm sorry."

"Nothing to be sorry about," Vince assured her, shaking his head. "It's just—"

He paused and pursed his lips. She didn't speak, but her expression was open and caring, so he continued.

"My mom always fussed over Nate and me. Now Nate has Jessica to care for him. It makes me more aware than ever that I don't have anyone like that in my life."

"You're lucky that you had her," she whispered. "I never had anyone who cared enough to fuss over me. Not in my whole life."

"No one?"

She looked away, her gaze taking on a distant quality. He hoped he hadn't stuck his foot in his mouth and inadvertently hurt her with his words. He felt like a heel, and Melanie's emotional withdrawal only highlighted his mistakes.

He noticed her hand was still resting on the gear shift. Her skin looked soft and delicate, reminding Vince once again that he shouldn't make sweeping judgments about someone before getting to know them first. Holding his breath, he took what was maybe the biggest risk of his whole life—he placed his hand over hers.

He thought she'd probably pull away, but she didn't. Instead she turned her hand over and squeezed his.

She'd obviously been through a lot in her lifetime, and he wondered why there'd been no one there to protect her and care for her. It went against every fiber of his being that someone or some circumstance had caused lasting inward scars on this outwardly beautiful woman, wounds that had stayed with her into adulthood. He silently prayed that her future would hold the love and peace she hadn't found in her childhood.

She still wouldn't look at him. The conversation had taken a much more personal tone than either of them had expected, and he sensed she was even more uncomfortable than he was with it.

He squeezed her hand one more time and, thinking to give her a moment of privacy in which to collect herself, he let himself out of the truck, struggling for a moment with his crutches before he found his balance.

As he approached what was left of the day care facility—which was nothing—Vince leaned heavily on his crutches and sighed. Despite the well wishes of the teenagers who approached him, he still felt the enormity of the burden before him. He'd come down with the intention of personally thanking the teens for all their assistance. Now he found himself wishing he could help them, even if it was just a little bit, and was frustrated by the fact that he was so confined by his stupid cast.

What was he going to do, kick around the ashes with his one good leg? A fat lot of help he was going to be.

He closed his eyes, wishing it all away. If only this were a bad dream and he would soon wake from his sleep. But of course when he opened his eyes again, nothing had changed.

Reality check.

The fire had consumed every inch of the building and every bit of the equipment that had been inside. It was all gone. Completely and utterly destroyed, turned into bags upon bags of worthless debris in the blink of an eye.

And yet it could have been so much worse, he reminded himself. He had much to thank God for.

None of the kids had been hurt. Or his brother. Or Gracie. Or Jessica.

People couldn't be replaced. Buildings could.

Except in this case, Vince didn't know when it would happen. Or more to the point, *how*. The ministry was barely making it financially as it was. There'd been no way to predict such a disaster, and even if he had, his budget constraints wouldn't have been able to have changed much.

He sighed again and made absent circles in the ash with the end of one of his crutches. He heard Melanie exit the truck and slam the door shut, but he didn't turn to look at her as she approached.

Instead, he closed his eyes once again, this time centering his heart on heaven and the throne of grace. Silently, he pleaded with God for the strength and wisdom to deal with this new trial.

Most of all, he prayed for the faith to believe God would get him through this, for he had never felt as utterly alone and abandoned as he did at this moment.

In his head, he knew he couldn't let his feelings dictate his faith, but his heart was not so quick to catch up.

"What are you doing?" Melanie asked, abruptly putting an end to Vince's agonizing prayer.

Reluctantly, he opened his eyes and turned to face her. "Praying."

Her copper-penny eyes widened noticeably.

"Seriously? I thought maybe you were looking for something there in the ashes."

"In a way, I guess I was," he answered with a twisted smile. "Guidance."

Melanie shook her head. "Excuse me?"

"From the Lord."

She didn't look convinced. Her right eyebrow twitched upward in that compelling way she had, and then her eyes narrowed and she locked her gaze on him. He fought with a powerful urge to look away from her and, with effort, managed to maintain eye contact with her.

"I hope I don't sound insensitive, but it seems to me this place needs a lot more than a prayer."

"I'll do what I can," Vince replied softly, thinking of how little he *could* do. There wasn't enough money to renovate, much less rebuild.

Her gaze widened, but she didn't speak.

"As I can," he continued. "When all is said and done, asking God for guidance is the first and most important thing I can—and should—do."

And the only thing he could *do right now,* he added silently. He was out of options, humanly speaking, anyway.

"I'm curious," she said, "what you think God is going to do for you. He didn't stop the fire from happening. Why do you think He's going to help you now?"

He winced internally, but hoped it didn't show on his expression.

"You don't sound like you believe in God," he commented in a low tone. "Do you?"

Vince knew the exact moment Melanie shut down. He thought he glimpsed a moment of anger before the steel barrier dropped over her eyes and her expression became blank and neutral.

"If you mean the big guy in the sky who tosses out thunderbolts to fry all of us poor sinners every time we do something wrong, then no. I don't believe in God."

She tried to make it sound like a joke, but Vince didn't buy that for an instant. She'd unconsciously crossed her arms in front of her and was standing defensively, whether she realized it or not. She clearly had unresolved issues in her life, but what that had to do with her belief in—or in this case, animosity toward—God, he couldn't guess.

His heart hurt for her. Even with the awkwardness of his crutches and his cast, he very much wanted to reach out to her, maybe give her a reassuring hug, but something held him back. Maybe it was that he couldn't quite let himself forget that she didn't like him very much to begin with, and nothing they'd talked about recently would have done much to have changed her opinion about him.

He gripped the handles of his crutches until he'd tempered the need to comfort her, knowing it would probably only distress her further.

"This may sound a bit cliché, Melanie, but God is love," he commented softly.

She snorted and shook her head adamantly. "Yeah. I've heard that before. I'm not buying."

Vince wondered just what she *had* heard and from whom. Certainly she hadn't been exposed to Jesus, the loving and forgiving Savior whose Spirit Vince carried within his own heart.

"Anyway," she continued, "I haven't been struck down by lightning yet. I guess that counts for something."

There was no way to counter that statement— either *yes* or *no* would put him in equally hot water—so he changed the subject, vowing silently that by the end of the six weeks of their acquaintance, he would find out the truth about

Melanie Frazer; and hopefully, he prayed, she would find out the truth about God.

"This is pretty much a disaster," he said, gesturing across the piles of blackened ash with his crutch. "The truth is, I don't have the money to rebuild."

Brilliant. Not exactly the smoothest change of subject in the history of the world.

He only now realized how foolish it was to lay out his financial troubles out to the very person who'd been hired to *change* everything. He'd been thinking of Melanie as a woman and not as a business consultant, and hadn't even considered that he might later come to regret what he was telling her.

Way to get in hot water.

Chapter Five

Melanie was quiet for a moment as her gaze lingered where Vince had pointed. The stark ruin called up something in her that made her throat tighten painfully. Maybe it was a sense of empathy for a man who'd clearly lost a great deal.

"I don't understand," she admitted softly. "I thought—that is, I was under the impression—that Morningway Lodge is very successful. Are you having problems attracting guests? I should think this idyllic mountain setting would have people clamoring to make reservations."

Vince shrugged and nodded. "Actually, we have a waiting list."

"But?" she prompted, when Vince did not immediately continue.

"But the truth is. we barely make ends meet

from month to month. I suppose you're going to find out sooner or later, what with you hovering over my books. Money issues are probably my biggest challenge." His voice had once again taken on the defensive tenor Melanie was used to hearing from him, and she half regretted asking. For a moment there, they'd been getting along, and it had been nice. Or at least somewhat of a relief for her.

But she couldn't help if she didn't know, so she plunged ahead.

"Maybe you should raise your rates," she replied jauntily. She was only half kidding. Surely he'd already thought about that option, as it was the most obvious quick fix to his problem.

"Not possible," he assured her. "The lodge is a ministry to the families of patients recovering at the Rocky Mountain Physical Rehabilitation Hospital just up the road. The hospital caters to those who've been paralyzed by an accident or other trauma. That alone is hard enough for the families to deal with, without adding the stress of trying to find a place locally where they can stay near their loved ones for a reasonable price."

"So you sometimes give them reduced rates, based on need," Melanie deducted.

Vince nodded. "Sometimes."

She arched her eyebrow.

"Okay. Often," he amended. "But these families need what the lodge has to offer, and I'm not about to turn them away. Money isn't everything. And God is faithful. My father started this ministry over twenty years ago, and we've always managed to pay our bills, one way or another."

But not this time.

He paused and although he didn't move a muscle, Melanie felt like his whole countenance slumped.

"I don't know how," he continued, shaking his head. "But between me and God, we'll work it out."

As soon as he said the words, a steely light touched his blue-eyed gaze and he thrust his chin an inch higher. The man was nothing if not determined, Melanie thought—maybe to a fault. He was too proud to ask for help, or even to accept it when it was offered to him.

But whatever the case, he was certainly not like any other man she'd ever known. On one hand, he was proclaiming God's faithfulness, yet on the other, he admitted he didn't know how he was going to be able to solve his problems.

His brand of faith and dependence on this apparently personal God of his was totally foreign to Melanie. He didn't throw God's weight around to get his way. He didn't yell or pout or threaten anyone when the going got tough and when he was faced with seemingly insurmountable problems.

He simply believed.

"There's nothing more to be done here," Vince said, his voice jagged. "We may as well head back to the lodge."

He gestured her back to the truck while he met briefly with the youth group leaders. Melanie got behind the wheel, waiting until Vince and his cast were situated before she turned the ignition.

She didn't speak. He seemed deeply preoccupied, and she didn't want to chatter at him. For all she knew, he was praying again.

She couldn't begin to comprehend the man. He was complicated and multifaceted, and she knew she had only scratched the surface of who he really was. However, she had learned one important thing about him today, some-thing that would no doubt help her in her quest to rework his business: Vince Morningway was probably the most generous man she'd ever met.

Letting people stay at the lodge even when they couldn't pay? Giving all his time and energy to a business model destined for fail-ure and yet which somehow had survived for twenty years?

Even today, he'd taken the time to speak with each teenager in the youth group individually, and he knew all their names; all this while mourning the loss of a vital part of the lodge. No one who saw him would ever know how much he was hurting just by watching him, but she knew. She'd seen the flittering expressions of angst and worry when he thought no one was looking. She'd seen him bow his head in prayer in the middle of a blackened heap of ash that stood where the day care used to be located.

When Vince said *ministry,* he meant it.

For most people she knew, men and women alike, it was all about the money. The success. The prestige.

For Vince, it was all about helping people.

* * *

The next morning when Melanie knocked on the door to Vince's office, there was little need for him to choose between a frown and a smile. He was grinning from the moment he heard her footsteps approaching. It was probably not the smartest way for him to react, given that the determined redhead was still on her mission to revamp his business, but he couldn't seem to be able to help himself.

He felt as jittery as a little kid on an awkward pair of skis who was facing his first bunny slope, and the way his heart slammed into his throat at his first sight of her should have set off warning sirens; but if it did, he was too flummoxed to notice.

If it wasn't for his cast, he might have jumped up to meet her at the door, but as it was, he valiantly endeavored to lunge in front of his desk to keep Melanie from seeing the disarray.

She stood in the door for a moment, her right eyebrow arching upward and a knowing smile on her face. Clearly she suspected something was up.

And it was. He'd come to the office two hours early this morning; partly because he couldn't sleep, and partly with the far-fetched notion that maybe he could somehow manage to rectify the current state of his filing system—if one could actually refer to his hodgepodge way of stuffing papers into the cabinet a *system*.

It was sound reasoning, to try to fix the issue before it *became* an issue. He didn't want Melanie going ballistic on him. If the files at least *appeared* orderly, maybe she'd leave them alone.

Leave *him* alone.

Only now he wasn't quite so certain about that last part. He wasn't so certain now that he didn't want to have her around; at least until he'd gotten to know her better. She was intriguing, to say the least.

Even so, he'd rather she didn't see how disorganized he was. especially with his filing system. He'd never before thought his office was in disarray. Now he knew it was, thanks to Melanie's keen eye.

"What's up?" she asked suspiciously. She stepped to one side, and he followed her movement, trying to block her from seeing inside the office.

Like that was going to work. She was going to see it sooner or later.

Unfortunately, all he'd managed to do with

his efforts this morning was create even more of a mess. At least before he'd started, the bevy of mismatched files had been *in* the filing cabinet. Now they were spread everywhere—his desk, the top of the filing cabinet, the credenza and every square inch of the floor. Not at all the impression he was trying to make.

Impression?

Vince took a mental step backward. Since when was he trying to make any kind of impression on Melanie? What he should be—*was*—trying to do was get himself out of the predicament Nate had forced him into.

He needed to keep his head in the game, especially when Melanie stepped sideways to peer over his shoulder.

"I'm hesitant to ask what you're doing, but I think I already know the answer to my own question," she said with a chuckle. She feinted to the right and then dodged to the left, moving so swiftly she was around Vince before he knew what she was up to.

Vince squared his shoulders and turned toward her. "Just tidying up my file cabinet."

"Yes," she replied, drawing out the word. "I can see that."

He folded his arms in front of him and leaned

his hip on the corner of the desk, taking the weight off his bad leg. He knew his defensive posture was not lost on Melanie, whose right brow did that cute little twitching thing again.

"How many years back do these files go?" she asked, picking up the folder closest to her. It was jammed with crumpled and folded pages. Vince had no idea what might be on them.

He shrugged complacently. "I have no idea. As long as I've been running the lodge maybe. Ten-plus years or so, I guess."

Her copper eyes widened and her jaw dropped. "Ten *years* of papers? All filed—using the term loosely—like this?"

"More or less." Definitely *more,* Vince thought, although he certainly wasn't going to admit that out loud.

"You have no idea how much I can do for you," she muttered, turning away from him. He could see her attention had gone from him to his messy desk, which was just as well. He hobbled a couple of paces around the desk and slid back into his chair. It put him back in Melanie's line of vision.

Not that she noticed.

Not that he *cared* if she noticed.

Her brow was wrinkled and her full lips were moving even though she wasn't speaking aloud. She'd pulled up the mismatched stack of files nearest to her and was dividing them into neat groups on her side of the desk. She paused every so often to straighten an errant corner or correct a crooked tab.

Vince leaned back in his chair and locked his hands behind his head. Maybe this wouldn't be so bad, her doing the work for him. And he thought it was cute the way she was obsessed with neatness and organization.

"You know, I think they have pills for that," he offered, when she had been working for a full five minutes without speaking a word to him.

She looked up, taking a moment to focus on him, as if she wasn't quite certain where she was. "Excuse me?"

"OCD," he prompted with a sly grin.

She looked about her at the orderly stacks and then back at him. She pointed at the files on his side of the desk, skewed every which way. He'd not touched them since she arrived. Who could blame him? He'd been distracted by the view of the good-looking woman across the desk from him.

"Unfortunately for you," she stated wryly, and then pursed her lips as if she were considering her next words. Or covering a smile. "There is no medical cure for chronic disorganization."

Her lips quivered, and then the smile she'd been struggling to contain emerged full force, followed by hearty, high-pitched laughter. It wasn't a polite chuckle, as Vince would have expected. She was downright enjoying herself, and within moments, Vince was laughing right along with her—a full-blown belly laugh that surprised him. He hadn't laughed so hard in as long as he could remember. Laughter just wasn't part of his job description.

"However," Melanie continued when she could speak, "where medical science fails, Melanie Frazer prevails. Once I'm finished, you'll be thanking that charming brother of yours for hiring me."

Her eyes were dancing with mirth and her mouth remained curved in a pretty smile. She was teasing him. Her words didn't have any real significance for her.

But for him, it was like being tried, sentenced and shackled in irons. The sizable weight on his shoulders, which had lifted momentarily when he was laughing with Melanie, slammed back down on him sevenfold. He almost winced, so intense was the heavy sensation. The air became stagnant and harsh to breathe.

His *charming brother.*

Everything always came back to Nate. For all of his life, whenever he and his brothers were compared with each other, Nate always won out. Why should he have thought Melanie would be the exception?

And why did her opinion matter anyway?

"I have other things to do around the lodge today," he said curtly. He pulled himself up and moved awkwardly toward the door to the office, hating that the crutches made him look less dignified. "You're welcome to stay here if you like."

Her smile wavered when she saw the stern look on his face and her eyes filled with concern. "I don't mind working alone," she assured him. "You go do whatever you need to do. I'll have your filing system into shape in no time. I can borrow a scanner from my office so we can archive the old stuff."

On the inside, Vince was struggling to maintain his composure, although he kept his expression cool and distant. He'd had it up to his neck with people meddling in his affairs—starting with Nate and ending with an intrusive redhead who was making a calamity of everything she touched.

Trying to fix his business—like it was broken. He might not be organized in the classic sense of the word, but he had a system, and it worked for him.

"Do whatever you want with the files," he snapped as he shuffled out the door, his back to her. "Origami, if the mood strikes you." He leaned on one crutch and pushed his glasses back up on the bridge of his nose. "Just don't involve me in it."

Chapter Six

Melanie sat without moving, pondering what she'd just witnessed. Something had set Vince off like the tail of a firecracker on the Fourth of July. His usually gentle, bright blue eyes had turned an indigo color—almost black—full of thunder and lightning; at least for the first few moments, after which he had reined his expression to carefully neutral. She could see from his clenched fists and the straining cords of muscle in his neck that he'd been struggling to hold his anger in check.

And this was all because she'd mentioned Nate's name.

No—she hadn't even done that. What had she said? She couldn't remember. She'd been speaking off the top of her head, not meaning anything by her words.

Intentional or not, Vince had been offended. He really, *really* didn't like his brother. She wasn't even certain he liked *her*, but that was a different subject entirely.

With a loud sigh, she dropped into Vince's office chair. It was the one piece of furniture in his office that was relatively new, and the plush leather cushioned around her.

Suddenly she felt like she couldn't move, and a feeling of mental claustrophobia thoroughly enveloped her senses as the chair had done with her body. It was as if her blood had turned to ice and her muscles to mud. Even her mind seemed to slow.

She held her breath for a moment to let the feeling pass. It was an old but familiar reaction to a man's anger, stemming from her childhood and potent even now.

But only if she let it bother her—and she wasn't going to do that. With effort, she forced those particular memories to the back of her consciousness, chained up and out of sight where they belonged.

She sighed as the stranglehold on her emotions loosened and cool, clean air filled her lungs. She needed a clear head to figure out what to do next. The project was challenging

enough without adding a good-looking, prin-
cipled and thoroughly exasperating man into
the mix.

She liked Vince. She really did. Even though
he didn't smile easily or often, he had kind eyes
and a smooth, gentle voice. He wasn't a brutal
or overbearing man, even when he was angry.
He'd been a little bit short with her maybe,
but it was a far cry from what she was used to
seeing in men when they got angry—yelling,
shouting, breaking things.

She'd fought with everything she had to make
something different and worthwhile of a life
that had seen too little beauty and warmth. She
had a successful career in a field she loved, and
she was content with that.

Relationships were too much work, and she
was the first to admit she'd never trust a man
long enough to really get close to him. It was
far better for her to be alone and feel like a
partial success than to be in a relationship and
feel like a complete failure.

Besides, she was about to receive a promotion she'd had her eye on for years. Which, she
thought wryly, was why she should be working,
and not mulling on things over which she had
no control.

With the strong-willed effort that had gotten her this far in life, she turned her mind to her work. A lesser woman would be overwhelmed by this project. Whatever Vince had been doing this morning, it wasn't creating any sort of logical filing system out of this jumbled mess of folders. How many years' worth of papers had he said he had lying around?

It wouldn't be a huge overstatement to say Vince had files stacked on nearly every flat surface. It was going to take quite some time to make sense of them. And it was just what she needed—a way to redirect her thoughts and stuff away her feelings.

The pile of folders in front of her was as good a place to start as any. She reached for the file on top and started rifling through the wrinkled papers.

It wasn't long before she was thoroughly engrossed in her work. So much so that she didn't hear Nate enter the office until he rapped his knuckles on the desk.

She jerked up, startled by his sudden presence. She hadn't realized he'd returned from Denver.

"Just the person I was looking for," Nate said with an easy smile.

Melanie shifted her weight, sitting back in the chair. Nate's posture was unassuming, but there was something fishy about the way he rubbed his hands together like an old merchant getting the good end of a bargain.

"What can I do for you?" she asked warily.

"I need help, and you're the best woman for the job," Nate said cryptically.

Melanie arched an eyebrow. This was old news, and she couldn't imagine why Nate was restating the obvious. She might have been slow out of the gate in getting the lodge's business practices where they needed to be, but she was making excellent progress now. At least she had many of the piles of folders in a semblance of order, and not strewn willy-nilly all over the room as Vince had done.

Unless Nate wasn't talking about the business.

"What job?" she asked cautiously, not quite sure what to expect. A warning bell rang in her head, and she heeded its call.

Nate laughed. "You can relax, Melanie. It's all good. I'm not asking much. There's just this one extra thing, and it will be easy enough for you to accomplish."

"Which is?"

"In a couple of weeks, there will be one specific day where I need to have Vince's full attention directed elsewhere than at what is going on about the lodge. It doesn't have to be much. Just a training session on the computer or something—anything so he doesn't see what I'm doing, and who is going in and out. I've got a great surprise planned for him, and I don't want him to know anything about it until it happens."

"I'm sorry, but no." Melanie didn't even skip a beat to draw a breath.

There was no question about whether she would help Nate with *anything* concerning Vince. Not with how Vince felt about his brother. Not a chance.

"Really? I thought you would help me." Nate gave her another one of his award-winning smiles, but he might as well have saved it. His friendly cajoling might work with most people, but it wasn't going to get him anywhere with Melanie.

"Babysitting isn't is my job description. I'm afraid you'll have to find someone else to help you." Someone else to be target practice for Vince when he found out people were carrying out some sort of *surprise* behind his back.

And most especially if that *someone* was trying to help Nate.

"I wouldn't ask this of you except you're the closest person to Vince right now, and you have the perfect excuse for diverting him. This is really important."

Nate had obviously changed tactics, but again, his plea was unsuccessful. She shook her head. She was here to reconcile Vince's business practices, not his relationship with his brother.

Melanie held up both hands, palms outward. She had heard enough. "Please, stop, Nate. Really. I don't even want to hear about it."

Nate looked like a little boy who'd dropped his ice-cream cone onto the hot cement, but Melanie would not be swayed.

Her presence in Vince's life wasn't personal, and it wasn't going to be. She was just now starting to make progress with her...work.

Right?

Yes. That was it. Her *work*.

Crow wasn't Vince's favorite delicacy, but he knew it was going to be the main course of his next meal. He was ashamed of the way he had treated Melanie the day before. It wasn't like him to be downright rude—but when it came to Nate, Vince lost his usual stringent restraint.

He'd thought he'd see her in his office bright and early in the morning as she had been on previous days, but she was nowhere to be found. He immediately noticed how much progress she'd made on his office, and when he found a large pile of folders marked *To be scanned,* he remembered she'd mentioned bringing up a portable scanner from her office in Boulder.

He wished he could have just offered to buy one and saved her the hassle of borrowing a scanner from work, but that was one more expense the lodge didn't need right now, and Vince was relatively positive he'd never use the machine at all once Melanie was gone.

With Melanie out, presumably for the day, Vince simply pushed a pile of folders aside to make working space on his desk and went back to working through his usual endless stream of paperwork.

Before he knew it, it was mid-afternoon. The sun was already slanting well toward the west, promising a colorful Colorado sunset in an array of pastels. And still no Melanie.

Thinking she should have returned to the

lodge by now, he hobbled down the hallway to her room. He rapped twice on the door, and then again when she didn't answer, but all remained quiet. Curious. It wouldn't have taken her an entire day just to grab a scanner from her office. Guilt gnawed at his stomach. Was it possible he'd actually scared her away from the lodge for good?

He frowned as he reluctantly acknowledged a new and startling self-revelation.

He didn't want her to leave. And not because of the business.

He was attracted to Melanie in a way he couldn't explain, even to himself. Something about her just drew him in like a fisherman reeling in a trout on a hook.

He was keenly aware that he was vacillating like a yo-yo. Yesterday he wanted her gone. Today he hoped she would stay.

He needed a plan. He would have to change if he wanted to keep her around, assuming that she ever came back.

Six weeks. That was what she had told him. At first, it had seemed like forever. Now it wasn't nearly long enough. The first week was sweeping by him like an early spring thunderstorm, and he was helpless to hold it back.

What he could do—what he *should* do, he suddenly realized—was show her the other part of his work, the stuff he did when he wasn't sitting behind a desk.

The part that really made a difference in people's lives. Even though sometimes it seemed to him that his entire existence was an endless string of paperwork and phone calls, there was much more to the ministry of the lodge, and to him personally.

To his heart.

Originally Melanie had planned to slip into the building, grab the scanner from her office and immediately return to the lodge. But she was feeling restless and a little bit uncomfortable after her last encounter with Vince, and there were a couple of dozen phone messages pinned neatly on one corner of her desk, so she had decided to take the afternoon away from the lodge to return her calls and—more importantly—regain her equilibrium.

What was it about Vince that made her feel vulnerable? Whatever it was, she didn't like it. There was no way she was going to let any man break through the armor she'd built around her heart. She knew all too well where that led, and she wanted none of it.

In truth, she doubted Vince would miss her—if he even noticed she wasn't around. And if he *did* notice, he was probably sighing in relief not to have a meddling busybody hanging over his shoulder and, as he saw it, criticizing every part of his life's work.

"I didn't expect to see you here," said her boss as she peeked into Melanie's office. Joan Whittaker was her immediate superior and her friend.

"I thought you were in the middle of a nice, cushy vacation in the mountains," Joan said.

Melanie shrugged and smiled. "I wouldn't exactly call it cushy. I had to trade in my heels for hiking boots."

"Oh, roughing it, are we?" Joan teased. "Visiting a nice quiet lodge in the mountains, surrounded by nature? I feel so sorry for you."

"You would if you met Vince," Melanie muttered under her breath.

Her complaint wasn't exactly meant to be heard, but Joan quickly picked up on it. "Vince Morningway? The guy you're working for? What's the problem?"

"*He's* the problem," Melanie barked, then

pinched her lips together and gazed out the window. "Sorry. It's just that I get riled up just thinking about that man."

"Ooooh!" Joan exclaimed, drawing out the word and sounding very much as if she'd just found a chest teeming with buried treasure. She pulled up a chair and leaned over the desk.

"Tell me all about him," she whispered conspiratorially, barely containing her enthusiasm. "I want details."

Melanie's eyebrows hit her hairline and her jaw dropped.

"There aren't any details. At least not the kind you mean."

"No?" her friend ribbed. "I think there *are* details. Spill it, girlfriend. You know I'm not going to stop pestering you until you tell me, so you might as well give up now."

Melanie sighed dramatically. Joan was right on both counts. Her friend wouldn't stop nagging, and Vince was quickly becoming a personal problem. Maybe it would help to talk about it.

"Let's just say he isn't the easiest person to work with, and leave it at that."

Of course it was too much to hope Joan would do anything of the sort.

"How so?"

"For starters, he didn't even know I was coming out to help him. His brother hired our firm and didn't tell Vince about it until I showed up at the lodge unannounced."

Joan laughed. "How did that work out for you?"

"He is not happy I'm there."

"Then why are you staying?"

The answer might have been as simple as the fact that Vince had been outmaneuvered by his father and brother, but if she were being honest, it was much more than that.

"He needs my help," she said at last. "I've never met a man as chronically disorganized as he is. His computer sits on the back credenza gathering dust while he struggles through his financials by hand. And don't get me started on his so-called filing system. He's a wreck."

"And he's gorgeous," Joan guessed, one corner of her lips rising suggestively.

"What?" Melanie squawked, caught completely off guard by her friend's comment. Her heart rate soared and she guessed her face was turning as red as her hair. She could feel the warmth of the blush rising over her chin and cheeks.

"Try to sit there and tell me he's not one fine-looking man," Joan prodded.

"I haven't noticed," she responded, sniffing as if she were affronted by the comment.

"Of course not," Joan said. "So you wouldn't be able to tell me what color his eyes are, then, would you?"

"Bright blue," she said without thinking, and then realized she'd said the words aloud. Her face turned from warm to fiery hot in one instant.

Joan puffed up like a rooster in a hen-house. Melanie put a hand over her eyes and groaned.

"So you *have* noticed him. Why do I suspect that he is the real problem here?" Joan asked, suddenly gentle but openly curious. "I don't think I've ever seen you shaken up by a man before. That's *my* department."

Melanie was relieved that her friend treaded lightly on the subject. She was so embarrassed that she felt like she was about to turn into liquid and melt into a puddle on the floor.

"Yes, I guess I am flustered by the man. So what do I do now?" she asked. "Because you're the expert, I mean."

She hoped her teasing tone would make the

question sound casual, although it was anything but. Melanie's track record with men wasn't bad. It was nonexistent, and she liked it that way. At least, she thought she did.

Until now.

"What do you do?" Joan repeated, sounding slightly amused. "Stop dragging your feet and get back to the lodge, that's what. Flirt with him a little and see where it takes you. He sounds like he's pretty entrenched in his work, so you're going to have to give him a hint about how you feel."

"I don't *know* how I feel," Melanie countered. "And even if I did, I wouldn't tell Vince. He doesn't even like me."

Joan laughed. "I may not know Vince personally, but I know men. Sweetie, you have a lot to offer—beauty and brains. He'd be a flaming idiot not to notice you."

"I think *I'm* the idiot," she responded, sighing deeply. "For noticing him."

Chapter Seven

It had been good, Melanie reflected, to have taken the trip back to Boulder to get a scanner for Vince's files, clear her head and talk with Joan. Yet by the end of the day, Melanie had found herself missing the cool mountain air and the quaintness of the lodge nestled up in the pines, which honestly surprised her. The bustle and pace of Boulder, with its college students biking to and from their classes and businesspeople milling to and from work, had always appealed to Melanie. She considered herself a one-hundred-percent city girl.

But there was something to be said for the majesty surrounding Morningway Lodge, and the comforting, cozy feeling of being snuggled within the deep, sparkling, snow-covered forest range. She had to admit it was a nice change of pace to breathe fresh, clean air. The scent of the pine trees pervaded the area even before the initiation of spring, and the evergreens were a lovely, colorful contrast to the glaze of the snow.

The little corner of the world that was Morningway Lodge was completely foreign to Melanie, yet it somehow cried out to her in the deepest recesses of her soul; suggesting something more, something missing from her life. It was a profound ache to which she could not put a name.

It was late by the time she arrived back at the lodge and went straight to bed, her mind still humming with unanswered questions; or at least the unsettling feeling that she had questions to ask but didn't yet know what they were.

By the next morning, Melanie was anxious to get back to work, and even though she anticipated the task of scanning mountains of pages into an electronic format to be somewhat tedious, Melanie found something oddly comforting about putting things into order, and she didn't really mind the job.

And Vince would be there. She didn't know if that was a good thing or a bad thing.

Maybe both.

She had absented herself the day before without checking with him, mainly because she wasn't sure if he wanted to see her. She wasn't sure even now, but she was more determined than ever to make a success of this project and move forward with her career plans. Whatever misplaced attraction she had for Vince was no doubt only a surface reaction. He *was* good-looking in his own way. That must be what was making her heart flutter like a spring butterfly.

It simply couldn't run deeper than that.

Or could it?

Why was she thinking this way? It could only lead to trouble.

She reached for the knob to Vince's office door and then paused, drawing in a deep breath for courage. She didn't know why she was nervous, but she certainly wasn't going to let an odd-tempered, surly man intimidate her. If he had problems, they didn't involve her.

And her problems did *not* involve him.

To her surprise, Vince wasn't sitting at the desk as she entered. He was standing in front of the desk, a pencil tucked behind his ear and his hair, for once, neatly combed. His face was animated and his lips were moving, though she couldn't make out what he was saying. He was obviously speaking to someone standing behind the door where Melanie couldn't see.

Unfortunately, she was already halfway through the door before she realized Vince wasn't alone. Even more regrettable was the fact that he had already seen her. He turned his head upward, meeting her gaze with his bright blue eyes and nodding as if he'd expected her all along.

"Excuse me," she said immediately, backing out of the doorway. "I didn't know you had company, Vince. I should have knocked."

"Melanie," Vince said with a smile. His voice was warm and kind, the same tenor he used when he was speaking to his little niece, Gracie. "Come on in. We've been waiting for you."

Curious, Melanie straightened and stepped forward. The person Vince had been talking to was an older man in an electric wheelchair. Vince had pushed the office chairs back to the wall, allowing extra room so the man could freely move his chair around.

It was immediately obvious to Melanie that the two men were related. Although the older man had obviously been hit with the ravages of some disease, his eyes still shone brightly and intelligently at her. The way his gray hair stood on end reminded her very much of Vince, as did the square jaw and—yes. there was a cute little dimple right there in the middle of his chin. Just like Vince.

Melanie didn't wait for Vince to introduce her to his father. Instead, she smiled and reached out her hand to the man.

"You must be Vince's father," she said, taking more than an educated guess.

"Guilty as charged, young lady," the man replied. "Jason Morningway, at your service."

"Melanie Frazer," she responded, smiling. "You have a beautiful place here. I'm really enjoying my time at the lodge."

That wasn't a complete lie, but she didn't dare look at Vince when she said it.

Out of the corner of her eye, she watched as Vince leaned his hip on the desk and crossed his arms. His lips quirked as if he were holding back a laugh.

"We're on the way to the hospital."

"Hospital?" Melanie asked, alarm piercing through her. "Is everything okay?"

"Oh, yes," Jason assured her. "Unfortunately,

a severe stroke put me in a wheelchair, so now I'm supposed to have physical therapy three times a week. Up until recently, Vince was always the one to drive me there. But since he broke his leg, Nate or Jessica have had to take me."

"But not today," Vince said, looking straight at Melanie. "Today, you're driving."

Driving?

With Vince's cast and his father's wheelchair, she sure wouldn't be driving her own car, which meant she'd have to drive Vince's truck. It was bad enough that she'd bounced Vince around the other day. But what horrible things might she do to his father with her poor mountain driving skills? She'd be mortified if she so much as hit a bump.

And there were lots and *lots* of ruts on the way to the hospital.

Vince was as nervous as he'd ever been in his life. He was about to show Melanie the deepest, most important part of his existence, something he'd never before shared with anyone but his family, and even they knew very little about what he did when he visited the hospital.

This was his passion. His heart.

And Melanie could reject it.

Reject *him*.

It was a risk he wasn't absolutely certain he wanted to take, but it was too late to back out now. He'd just jumped right out of the proverbial frying pan and into the flaming fire. Or rather, into the cramped backseat of his dual-cab truck, and that was no easy feat.

Not only that, but he was torturing poor Melanie. On purpose—sort of. He didn't really see any other way around it. His father couldn't drive the stick shift in his condition, and he surely couldn't. Which left Melanie by default.

He'd known how distressed she was driving him around the other day, afraid she was going to hurt him every time she hit a bump in the road. The woman had an incredibly sensitive heart underneath that independent exterior. He'd had several glimpses of it in the past few days, but especially when she'd been chauffeuring him to the day care site, all concerned about how her driving would affect his leg injury.

And now he'd put her in the same position, only this time it was Pop sitting in the front seat, chatting amicably with Melanie while she stared forward, both hands gripping the wheel and her jaw tight. Vince wondered if his father noticed he was the only one doing the talking.

"Sorry. Sorry," Melanie offered as they went over a particularly bad groove in the road.

"Will you stop it with the apologizing already?" Vince said with a laugh. "We're grown men. You aren't going to hurt us, and neither is this road."

"I'm still not comfortable behind the wheel of this big old thing," Melanie said. "My little car drives nothing like this truck, I assure you."

Vince chuckled. "Your *little car* wouldn't make it on most of these back roads. Although I have to say I'd love to see what it could do on a stretch of straight highway."

"It would beat this old truck by a mile," she assured him.

"Smoother, too," he teased. He knew she wouldn't see his amused grin unless she looked in the rearview mirror, but that didn't stop him from smiling.

"Why do I feel like I'm missing the joke here?" Pop asked, shaking his head.

"Melanie doesn't like ruts," Vince said,

thinking more of his dull business routine than the ruts in the road.

"You'll figure it out pretty quickly if you hang around her for any length of time," Vince assured him.

"Oh, I plan to do that," his father teased, wriggling his eyebrows. "You know how I love the pretty ladies."

Vince laughed, but Melanie shook her head, and he could see the color rising on the back of her neck. Her skin tone was so light that it registered even the smallest change in shade. He imagined her cheeks were stained a bright crimson as a result of his father's teasing, and wondered why that would be.

She wasn't the self-conscious type at all. She was strong and independent, and definitely not afraid to voice her opinions. Yet his father's mild flirtation had shaken her up somehow.

But only for a moment. As Vince considered what he could say or do to break the sudden tension he imagined she was feeling, Melanie broke into laughter.

"I knew the moment I walked into the lodge that you Morningway men would be nothing but trouble."

"You've got that right," Pop agreed. "I'm not too much of a threat, but you'd better watch out for my son here. He's just like a mountain lion. Steady and quiet, but as dangerous as can be. You've been warned," said Jason.

This time it was Vince's face that burned. He was glad he was sitting in the backseat where no one could see it. It was one thing for his father to flirt with Melanie. It was quite another for him to bring Vince into it.

A mountain lion? What on earth was his father talking about? He opened his mouth to speak and then closed it again, realizing he didn't have anything to say.

Melanie, however, didn't appear to be having that problem. "Mountain lion, huh? Well, don't worry about me. I assure you I've got Vince on my radar."

Pop looked at Melanie with wide eyes and a new interest, and Vince groaned softly. This was going from bad to worse in a matter of seconds, and he was right in the middle of it, even if he was in the backseat. In some ways it felt like they were talking about him as if he were not there; in other ways, it seemed like he was sitting right between them, a net for their volleying conversation.

He gritted his teeth, waiting for the moment the ball hit him square in the head and knocked him clean out.

The hospital wasn't far from Morningway Lodge, and once Melanie got on the paved highway, she had no trouble driving. Jason kept up the bulk of the conversation, in part, Melanie thought, to make her feel at ease.

She was grateful for his kindness, and it did help. Jason was friendly, open and easy to talk to; though his son, not so much. Vince barely added anything to the conversation, unless he was directly addressed, and that was not often—and only from his father, because Melanie couldn't think of a single thing to say to him.

Over the past week, there were times, at least, where Melanie thought she and Vince had broken some emotional barriers, going beyond just a polite acquaintance and into some sort of depth of a relationship, even if she didn't fully understand what that was. Now she felt like he'd closed himself off again, and Melanie wondered why. He appeared comfortable enough with his father, and it wasn't like Nate was around.

She didn't have much time to consider the answer to that question, or how she would overcome those barriers. One more ridge and the hospital was before them.

It was a large, modern facility that stretched out over the land, looking strangely at odds with the tree-filled, snow-covered mountain backdrop.

But then what had she expected, a log cabin with a shingle hanging out front?

During the drive, Jason had given Melanie a little background on the hospital, which she found of great interest, especially as it related to the Morningways. As she pulled up to the front of the building and parked the truck, she ran through some of the details in her mind.

The Rocky Mountain Physical Rehabilitation Hospital had originally been built in the late eighties as a long-term facility for those patients who'd been paralyzed for one reason or the other and who needed to learn the life skills necessary to live productive lives in the outside world. The majority of patients were victims of some kind of accident, although some had been hit with a physical ailment which left them equally incapacitated, like the stroke Jason Morningway had recently experienced.

At the time the hospital was built, Jason explained, he and Vince's mother were considering opening a bed and breakfast facility in the vicinity of Estes Park, more as a business than as a ministry.

Once they'd learned about the new hospital, though, God had moved their hearts to open up the lodge instead, making the hospital facility especially accessible to the families of the patients residing there. It had grown from that original small seed into Morningway Lodge as it was now, which, Melanie mused, had turned out to be much more of a ministry than a business endeavor.

Apparently, Jason wanted it that way, despite the fact that they weren't making any real profit on the business. Vince seemed to feel the same way, even though she couldn't imagine why. He'd inherited a ton of responsibility with no real perks that Melanie could see. It was no wonder he looked frazzled all the time.

As for Melanie, a month ago, she would have thought the very idea of such a ministry was crazy, not to mention just not good business sense. Everything in her rebelled at the very notion.

But now, she wasn't so sure how she felt.

Her head was telling her one thing, but her heart was telling her something different altogether.

Chapter Eight

Melanie held the electric wheelchair steady while Vince helped his father into it, and then Vince shifted to his father's left while Melanie walked on the other side, both slowing their steps to stay even with Jason. No one spoke as they entered the building. It was one of those moments when silence seemed to be instinctive.

Vince obviously knew just where he was going, and though he called a greeting to the woman behind the front desk, he didn't pause to speak with her at any length. Melanie inhaled the sharp, sterile scent she associated with medical facilities and cringed. It was all a bit overwhelming to her, to every one of her senses.

The hospital had several wings, and she

was beginning to feel they'd visited all of them before they entered an expansive, well-lit area.

The room was teeming with both people and objects—every kind of exercise equipment Melanie could conceive of and many she'd never seen before. There were benches and tables and two sets of parallel bars—one for adults and one that looked as if it were sized for children.

She was surprised at how busy it was. She didn't know exactly what she expected, but not this big of a group. The room was fairly buzzing with voices. Many of the people, both children and adults, were obviously residents of the hospital; for every patient Melanie observed, there was at least one scrub-clothed therapist at his or her side.

A pretty young lady immediately approached them as they entered. She had short black hair with spiky tips poking in every direction, and she was dressed in lavender scrubs. She wasted no time with introductions, but edged between Vince and the wheelchair and began turning Jason away.

"Timewise, you were down to the wire today," the therapist said with a chuckle. She poked Vince's father in the shoulder. "It isn't like you to be late, Jason."

"I'm not late," Jason growled back at her, although his expression was friendly and openly belied his words. "Your watch must be set too early, Rosemary. Besides, if I did happen to be running a few minutes late, I had a good reason. I've been doubly blessed in the *lovely ladies* department on this particular day. You can't blame me if I want to take my time about it."

He winked at Rosemary and nudged his chin toward Melanie. "One. Two. And I'm actively looking out for gorgeous gal number three. You know the old saying, *Good things come in threes?*"

Melanie felt a little flustered, but Rosemary simply brushed off the compliment as if she was used to it and herded a protesting Jason away from Vince and Melanie.

"Heartbreaker," she heard Rosemary quip.

"Slave driver," Jason retorted.

Melanie chuckled at their banter, but even laughter didn't quell her apprehension. Rosemary might be used to avid male attention, but Melanie definitely wasn't.

She'd never met such an openly flirtatious

man Jason Morningway's age. He said the most outrageous things, and she wasn't quite sure when to take him seriously, and when he was simply teasing her.

The father was certainly nothing like his son. She couldn't imagine Vince flirting with her that way.

Flirting at all, really. He wasn't the type.

She looked to Vince, who was standing squarely with one hand tucked in the pockets of his jeans and the other clutching the cane that he insisted on switching to, saying his crutches were too cumbersome. Melanie wasn't sure that was a good idea, but there was little she could do to dissuade him when he had his mind set on something.

He cocked his head a little to one side, his gaze focused on the way his father was being coerced toward a menacing-looking exercise machine. Half of a smile lingered on one side of his thin, masculine lips, and without thought she stared at him, wondering what he was thinking.

Suddenly his attention shifted, as did his gaze.

He was looking right at her.

He raised his eyebrows over the top rim of

his glasses, and the quirk of his cheek left her in no doubt that he was completely aware she was gawking at him, although his expression didn't give away the least idea of what he might be thinking.

Heat rose to her face and she knew her cheeks were turning a disastrous color of red, but she didn't look away. Rather, she tipped her chin up and looked right into his bright blue eyes, which were extra luminescent through his glasses, and sparkling with mischief and mirth.

"See anything you like?" he joked, his smile growing to full stature.

She did. She was suddenly and vibrantly aware of Vince as a man—a very attractive man.

"Don't you wish," she goaded.

"Maybe."

Maybe? That wasn't exactly a compliment, but then, she wasn't fishing for admiration. Was she?

"So…what are we going to do while your father is tortured?" She asked, changing the subject. She'd never experienced it herself, but she knew enough about physical therapy to know it wasn't a pleasant experience.

Vince chuckled. "You got that, did you?"

"From that gleam in Rosemary's eyes, I would say your father is in for it big time."

"He is, and trust me, he'll be complaining about it all the way home. In truth, though, he likes Rosemary, even if she's tough on him."

"Should we be waiting in the hallway?" she offered. She really didn't feel comfortable standing in the therapy room doing nothing.

"No, no. I figured I could show you around the hospital while my pop is busy with his visit," he said, sounding suddenly eager. "Sound good to you?"

Melanie nodded, harvesting some of his enthusiasm. "Sure. I'd like that."

He gestured her forward, walking beside her, his cane marking time with each step, while his free hand rested lightly on the small of her back, presumably to guide her. Vince was nothing if not polite.

That wasn't what was bothering her. She was suddenly and remarkably aware of his closeness—the musky, leathery scent of Stetson aftershave; the way their shoulders almost, but not quite, brushed each other as they walked. It was a palpable, thoroughly pleasant and completely alarming sensation, and Melanie didn't know whether to lean in and enjoy the moment or to slip away from him and hope the giddy feeling would pass on its own.

She was surprised when Vince led her through the room, rather than out the way they'd come in. In a quiet, smooth baritone, he spoke kindly to each patient he passed and jested with many of the physical therapists. It seemed to Melanie that he knew everyone by name, and conversely, that everyone knew him well. She added that fact to her mental personality profile, surprised at how much she'd modified her opinion of him since the moment they'd first met.

She'd initially read Vince as reserved and diffident, the type of man who wanted to be alone and who might eschew large crowds in favor of solitude.

Now she wasn't so sure. He clearly had formed relationships here at the hospital—with both patients and doctors. When he was interacting with them, his usual reserve went right out the door.

She was mulling over this new information when a large, daunting-looking man who was propped up to a forth-five-degree angle on a physician's table called out to Vince.

"Tell this guy to leave me alone," the giant man demanded with a menacing scowl, pointing at the physical therapist, who continued massaging the big man's calves as if he hadn't spoken at all.

Vince moved forward intently, his cane thudding with every other step. Melanie held her breath, wondering how Vince thought he might be able to intercede, and knowing instinctively that he planned to do so.

Because he cared.

The hair stood up on her arms. The man was intimidating even reclining on a table. He had more hair on his face than he had on his head, and he had the enormous physical bearing and attitude of a bouncer at a concert, with the personality and booming voice to match.

For a moment, Vince glared hard at the man, his mouth turned into a deep frown.

Before Melanie could blink, the frown disappeared, and Vince clasped the man's hand and leaned down to bump his shoulder in a welcome Melanie recognized as a familiar-yet-odd male greeting ritual.

"How are you, Bennett? Still making trouble for everyone who crosses your path?"

Although the question was clearly directed to

the patient, the physical therapist grunted and nodded, and the big man belted out a laugh.

"I have to keep these guys on their toes so they don't get lazy." His mouth twisted and Melanie glimpsed a sudden sadness in his eyes. "I just wish they could keep me on *my* toes, you know?"

The man's voice had grown softer as he finished his sentence. So did Vince's expression.

"Keep the faith," he said quietly.

The man winked. "You know it."

Vince introduced Bennett, whose first name was Frank, to Melanie, and then the two men spoke for a few minutes while the therapist worked.

"Time to change stations," the physical therapist announced.

Frank groaned and winked at Melanie. "I don't suppose you'd care to rescue me?"

Melanie stumbled over her words. Frank was a genuinely nice guy, despite her first impression. But now that she'd seen the sadness behind the bravado, what did she do with that?

Address it or ignore it?

She flat out didn't know what to say, and it disturbed her. She'd never been exposed to anything that gave her such a severe and acute emotional response as what she'd seen today. She was overwhelmed with empathy for Frank and for all the others convalescing here.

She sighed in relief as Vince stepped toward her and briefly put a possessive arm around her shoulders. Her breath caught, and then she exhaled deeply.

"Like I would allow her to run off with the likes of you," Vince teased. "Besides, I haven't had the chance to show her around the hospital yet. You are only our first stopover of many."

"First and best," Frank joked.

"Very likely," Melanie agreed, smiling at the big man and glad she had finally found her voice. She was usually quick with a comeback, but not with Frank. She still didn't know whether it was his size or the fact that he was paralyzed that intimidated her.

Whatever it was, she needed to get a grip and get over it.

Now.

Chapter Nine

It sounded to Melanie like Vince had quite a comprehensive tour prepared for her. He used his cane to gesture her through another door, located at the back of the physical therapy room. It was a different hallway than the one they'd been in before, but it was equally quiet.

Vince's soft sigh broke the silence. "Frank there was in an auto accident a few months ago. Someone ran a red light and sideswiped his car on the driver's side. The car was totaled. He was blessed to make it out alive."

"And his legs?" Melanie asked softly, her heart welling with compassion for a man she didn't know. Tears burned behind her eyes, but with effort, she held them back.

"He's making progress. It's a long haul. He may eventually walk again." He stopped and cleared his throat. "Then again, maybe not. Fortunately for him, he has a devoted wife who stays at our lodge and visits him daily. Many of these people have no one."

"I'm beginning to see what you mean when you call Morningway Lodge a ministry," she admitted.

"Yeah?" He smiled crookedly.

She nodded, swallowing over the catch burning in her throat.

Vince stared at her a moment, then used his free hand to push his glasses up the bridge of his nose, an action Melanie now understood to be a physical gesture he used to mentally or emotionally disconnect, to distance himself from a situation. She thought she might have made him uncomfortable, so she let the subject drop.

"This way," he said, pointing with his cane once again. "I have a few more things I'd like to show you."

The next stop was an indoor pool, which was encased by a large plastic-looking dome ceiling that Melanie thought might be seasonal, opening to the fresh air and sunshine during the summer. At the beginning of February, with the mountains perpetually covered in—at the very least—several inches of snow, the dome was tightly shut, sealing in the warm mist that rose from the water.

The humidity in the room was markedly higher, and Melanie loosened the red knit scarf still tucked around her neck. The smell of chlorine permeated the room and made her nose itch.

The pool wasn't as crowded as the gym had been. There were only three patients in the water, each accompanied by an attendant. As before, Vince immediately moved forward, stepping so close to the edge of the pool that Melanie thought he might slip and fall in. It was as if he'd forgotten that one of his legs was in a cast.

Maybe he had.

But, Melanie quickly perceived, if he wasn't thinking of himself, it was with good reason. Whatever exercises had been going on before Vince entered the room were immediately halted as the patients, with their attendants' assistance, floated closer to Vince to exchange a few words with him.

After polite introductions all around, Melanie simply stood back and observed. She had never seen Vince so animated nor his smile so wide. Compassion and sympathy flooded through his bright, beautiful blue eyes, and he treated each individual with such respect that whatever suffering the patients endured seemed to be lifted somehow, just by his presence.

Whatever it was that he was doing for these people was bringing them joy, making their lives more bearable. He reached out to them physically, yet also with something else, something intangible. Not emotionally, although that was part of it. Rather, it was…?

She struggled to put a label on it.

Spiritual? It was a remarkable thing to see, even if she didn't understand it.

She might have felt left out, except that Vince's smile included her. Every one of her senses was full to overflowing, welling up so deeply and intensely in her chest that she could hardly breathe.

It appeared Vince had some sort of effect on her as well. How utterly unnerving.

"Sorry I took so long back there," he apologized as they returned to the long, curved hallway.

"Not at all," she said, shaking her head and meaning every word with all her heart. "What you did in there, with those patients, was…"

She paused, searching for the right word. "Well, it was beautiful."

His eyebrows rose, and he reached a hand out and brushed it across her cheek. He searched deeply within her gaze for a moment before turning his head away.

"Just a couple more stops, and then we'll return to Pop," he promised.

Melanie didn't even know how to express how much being here with him, sharing something close and personal to him, really meant to her. She had learned more about Vince in the last hour than she had in all the previous days put together.

What a difference it made in her perception of him, getting a glimpse into Vince's heart; a man who to this point had remained very much a mystery to her.

It changed everything. Nothing in her training on personality profiling had prepared her for this. She could no longer deny she was emotionally involved with the man, however he felt about it.

And it wasn't just Vince. Her heart was authentically moved by the plight of those suffering from paralysis, trying to rebuild their lives at this hospital. She didn't simply feel sorry for the patients here. It wasn't in her nature to stand aside and let the world pass her by.

She wanted to help somehow. She didn't have the slightest inclination of what exactly she could do, but she couldn't just leave the hospital as if she'd never been through the experience and met the wonderful patients here.

"The next area I'm going to show you is extra special to me," Vince said, reaching out his hand to slow her down. He smiled gently, but there was unspoken sorrow in his gaze. "It may also break your heart."

As they walked down the hallway, she noticed that he hung back just enough to be able to watch her without being obvious. She thought he was probably assessing her, trying to see how well she was handling all the things she'd seen.

She didn't blame him for being hesitant. She would be if she were in his place. It was a lot to ingest all at once, and even with a strong person, it could go either way—freaking out or pulling it together.

Melanie wasn't just strong, she was resilient. This time Vince had shared with her wasn't going to bounce back in his face. Rather, she was going to *give* back.

She tipped her chin up and squared her shoulders, lending her a straight, confident posture. Vince must have seen the change, for he suddenly matched his pace with hers.

"Is your leg bothering you?" she asked when she observed him leaning heavily on his cane with each step.

"I'm all right," he insisted.

"Maybe you should have stayed with crutches?" She tried to make it sound like a question, a mild suggestion, when really what it was was sound advice.

"Not a chance. They hinder me too much. I can't even move with those things."

"Still…" she started, but he shook his head firmly, and that was the end of the subject.

"Ladies first," he said as he beckoned to a glass door. The entire wall was glass actually, and it didn't take long for her to see why.

There were a dozen children at least, all of early elementary school age. They looked like a normal group of kids, playing with various toys spread throughout the room. Even the sound coming through the door was that which she'd heard any number of times coming from the neighborhood playground. It was the sound of cheerful, happy children, calling to one another in excited, high-pitched voices.

Only these children were in wheelchairs.

Vince was right. Her heart lurched into her throat at the scene. But that was nothing to what happened when she and Vince entered the room. One look at the man and every one of the children stopped their play to clamor around them—or rather, *him*.

Her heart snapped right in two.

"Mr. Vince! Mr. Vince!" The children were struggling to get close to their *Mr. Vince*. He crouched down as low as he could to be at eye level with them, even though his cast clearly hampered him. He spent several minutes acknowledging each child personally, laughing and talking with them, before he had the opportunity to bring Melanie in on the obviously happy reunion.

It was more apparent than ever that Vince was a frequent visitor to the hospital, and in particular, to the children's ward. The children clearly loved him, and even the nurses' faces were shining with delight.

And he did all this hospital work in addition

to running Morningway Lodge. No wonder the man looked perpetually overworked.

Except for now.

Kneeling down on his good knee and surrounded by the noisy children, all the heavy stress lines usually marring his handsome face nearly disappeared. She even noticed, for the first time, the feathering of laugh lines at the corners of his eyes. It was as if he'd taken off a mask and revealed a new face to her, something that matched the amazing personality she was only now discovering in Vince.

His smile was wide, his eyes gentle. One little girl gestured for him to come nearer, and as he bent his head over hers, she cupped her tiny hand around her lips and whispered a secret, just for him.

"Mr. Vince," said another little girl, wheeling forward with a large purple hardbound storybook under her arm. "Will you read to us? Please?"

"Well, I could," he answered gently, taking the book from her. "But I'll bet Miss Melanie would do a much better job than I would.

A dozen eager children's gazes turned expectantly to Melanie.

And suddenly, she knew what she was doing

here. There probably wasn't much she could do for a man like Frank Bennett, but read to the children?

That she could do.

She met Vince's gaze over the heads of the children. "I'm afraid I'm a little out of practice."

"They're going to love you," he assured her, handing the book up to her. "Let me get you a chair."

She was about to say she'd be happy to sit on the floor close to the children, when she realized the inherent wisdom in his offer. Reading time for normal children might well have been in a circle on the floor, but for these children, eye to eye would be sitting in a chair.

Vince seated her with great relish, making a big production out of it, as if they were on a fancy dinner date. He ended his performance with a bow, and the children giggled, making Melanie blush, especially when he winked at her. Here was a man she had once thought to be staid and stuck-in-the-mud, rolling right around in said mud simply to tickle the children's funny bones.

And it seemed to come easy to him, as natural as breathing. Who would have guessed that behind Vince's stern exterior was a heart of gold?

She may have made the mistake of misjudging him before, but no longer. He was helping others in a way she could hardly conceive of, and she suddenly experienced a tremendous desire to pay him back for allowing her such a personal glimpse into his life's work.

And then she remembered Nate. He'd mentioned something special, something that would mean a lot to Vince. She'd cut him off before he could go into any kind of detail.

Now she wanted to know. And if she could help, she would. She made a silent promise to herself to look up Nate as soon as she got back to the lodge, find out what his plans were and see if he still needed her help.

There was no way she could justify her feelings or her actions as being anything to do with the job she was doing for Morningway Lodge.

This would be for Vince.

"Are you going to read the story or stare at it?" Vince inquired, tapping the book that still lay face down on her lap.

"What? Oh, y-yes, of course," she stammered, blushing again at having been caught daydreaming—in front of a dozen eager children, no less.

She turned the book over and, after clearing her throat, read the title aloud. *"All-Time Favorite Princess Stories."*

The boys groaned as one, Vince included.

Melanie laughed. "Do you have any other choices?"

"Iron Man," one boy suggested.

"Trucks and Planes," said another.

The girls unenthusiastic reaction was enough to assure Melanie that neither one of those choices were going to work either.

Laughing, Vince stood and moved to the bookcase. "Let's see if we can compromise."

He tapped his finger against his chin and then ran it across the spines of several books, like a boy running a tree branch across a picket fence. He selected a slim volume and offered it to Melanie.

This one had black-and-white line drawings of a rabbit on the front.

"The Tale of Peter Rabbit," she read with a sigh of relief.

The children, both boys and girls, cheered at Vince's choice.

He really *did* know these children. And there

was no doubt—from the kind, almost fatherly gaze he dragged across the children as he sat down between them—that he loved them.

And they loved him.

Melanie finished *Peter Rabbit* and had been persuaded by the children to read a second book before Vince stood and announced that it was time for them to go, a declaration the children were not at all happy about, if the collective squalor of voices was anything to go by.

"Don't worry," he assured them, reaching out to pat a couple of the kids on the head. "I'll be back to see you in a couple of days."

"And Miss Melanie?" one towheaded little boy asked thoughtfully.

Vince glanced at Melanie a moment and paused, his lips drawing tight. "Why don't we all thank Miss Melanie for reading to us today?"

The deflection, while probably not obvious to the children, cut into Melanie like a knife. Of course, as far as Vince was concerned, this was her one and only visit to the hospital. He couldn't know that she was already planning in her head how she would be able to schedule weekly appointments to come visit this ward and read to these precious children.

She smiled secretly. Vince didn't need to know. This was between her and the children. If she happened to run into Vince here at some time in the future, well, she supposed he would find out then.

"Where are the children's parents?" she asked when they'd walked some distance away from the playroom.

"Mostly, they stay at the lodge. The children, maybe more than anyone else, need to be near their loved ones—their parents—while they get well."

"And the parents, they visit the children here?" she asked. There hadn't been any parents in with the children she'd just seen. Only nurses.

"Yes. I planned to show you the dayroom where families spend time together, and then we'll go and pick up Pop." He glanced at his watch. "His physical therapy session should be almost finished by now."

She smiled, but inside, she was sorry the tour had to end so soon. Her mind was overwhelmed by all she'd seen and heard today, and that was nothing compared to her emotional state, but she found she wanted to learn more—about the hospital and about Vince.

Vince sensed Melanie's need to quietly absorb the impact of everything he'd shown her today, so he didn't try to make small talk as they moved from one corridor to the next. Instead, he focused his attention on the rhythmical tap of his cane on the concrete floor.

Thump-step. Thump-step.

He hadn't originally meant for Melanie to see the whole picture of what the RMPR Hospital did; certainly not all in one day. His original intention was to take her straight to the dayroom, where she could meet some of the visitors staying at Morningway Lodge in the context of their family members, who were patients here at the hospital. In that context, she could have been exposed to the ministry he did without being overwhelmed by it all.

But one thing had led to another, and within the hour, he'd more or less taken her on the grand tour—what would have been a normal round of visitation for him. Besides the dayroom, where they were now headed, there was only one other ward he usually visited—the special care unit, where patients with the worst injuries resided.

When he visited on his own, which was not usually during one of his father's appointments, he generally spent an hour or so praying with these special cases, people who would probably not get any better, not even with therapy. He wasn't ashamed of praying with these patients; on the contrary, he felt prayer was the best thing he could do for them.

There was another reason he hesitated to bring her to the special unit, and it wasn't because he didn't know if she could handle seeing the tough cases. From their few conversations about God and prayer, he had the distinct feeling Melanie wasn't comfortable with prayer. If he couldn't bring her into a prayer circle with these severely injured patients, she might feel ignored—or worse, offended. That definitely wasn't what he had in mind for sharing with her God's grace and love. She needed to hear it. Just not that way.

She had adapted very well to this visit, what with her outgoing personality and caring heart. But Vince knew this was due in part to the shot of adrenaline she'd probably experienced from her abrupt introduction into his world. Once that wore off, other, less welcome feelings might creep in, emotions he was well acquainted with but that he kept well in check.

Anger. Denial. Grief.

She'd seen more than enough heartache for one day.

He glanced at her, but she was staring straight ahead and was biting on the corner of her lip.

Lord, be with her, he prayed silently. It was a short prayer as prayers went, especially for Vince. Nate had often accused him of being long-winded, but what was there left to say? His whole soul was reaching upward to heaven, so much so that it was a physical ache deep in the pit of his stomach.

What if this was too much for her? If so, the blame would rest squarely on his shoulders.

Melanie was one of the strongest women he'd ever known, ranking right up there with his own mother, who had bravely fought her breast cancer until the end. Vince had been only eleven when she died, but the memory of her strength—and her faith—lingered with him still.

Melanie might not yet have faith in God, but she had strength.

Nevertheless, he was worried that her tender heart might be wounded by the visit.

He didn't realize he'd been walking ahead of her until he felt her hand on his arm.

He turned to her, concerned that his thoughts and worries for her might be, in fact, reality; even more so when he saw that her luminescent copper-penny eyes were glimmering with unshed tears.

And it was all his fault for bringing her here. How insensitive could one man be?

Instinctively he reached for her, experiencing a deep need to pull her into his arms and hold her close to him, to protect her and erase the sadness in her gaze.

With a soft groan, she stepped forward and wrapped her arms about his waist, holding on to him as if he were her lifeline. He held her tightly, laying his cheek against the top of her head. He closed his eyes and breathed in the fresh citrus scent of her shampoo, which he thought fit Melanie's personality perfectly.

"I'm sorry," he whispered raggedly in her ear. "I didn't think."

"Didn't think what?" Melanie asked, leaning back to see his eyes, but not stepping out of his arms.

He hadn't planned on elaborating. He simply

didn't *think,* and when Melanie's right eyebrow twitched upward, he lost whatever coherency he might have been able to gather to finish the sentence.

Any sentence.

His gaze dropped to the freckles brushing across her nose and cheeks, and he started counting them as a way to regain his focus. He was all the way up to seven when she reached up with both hands and outlined his jaw, forcing his gaze back to her eyes. They still glistened, but no tears had fallen.

Her eyes were a brilliant copper color. So wide. So beautiful.

And her gaze—sorrowful, yet filled with joy. Vulnerable, yet determined. There was so much to read in her eyes, so many emotions he saw but could not understand.

"I don't know if I will have the opportunity to say this later, so I'd better say it now." Her voice was soft but resolute.

Say what? He knew he hadn't spoken the words aloud, but they lingered in his mind. He swallowed hard. He couldn't have looked away from her if he'd tried.

"Thank you."

That was it. That was all she said.

Then her hands slid up to the back of his neck. She burrowed her fingers into his hair as she pulled his face closer to hers. She stood on tiptoe and sighed.

And then she kissed him.

Chapter Ten

The kiss was brief, soft and innocent. It ended before Vince could truly reciprocate, at least not the way he wanted to. His heart jolted and raced to such a speed that he experienced a weak-in-the-knees vertigo so strong that it had him clutching at his cane.

He might have kissed her again, to see if her lips were really as soft as they were in the memory which had instantly been branded in his mind, and to see if his heart fared any better on a second pass; but she had already stepped away and was concentrating fiercely on smoothing down the arms of her burnt-orange cable-knit sweater.

When she looked up, her gaze was polite but a little distant, which confused Vince, who felt like they had just shared something special and profound.

"Is there another long hallway, or are we almost there?" she asked. "I think I'm starting to get a little claustrophobic."

He shook his head, still reeling from the kiss. "No, it's just around the corner."

She nodded. "We should go, then," she said, her voice carefully modulated. "Your father will be waiting."

So that was how it was going to be. If they didn't acknowledge it, then it hadn't happened.

Vince closed up his own emotions even though it was more difficult for him to do so than it usually was. His brow creasing with the mental effort to go forward, he used his cane to gesture her onward. He greeted the nurses on duty, both of whom he knew by name. Beyond the desk was an open room that was at least three times the size of any other area of the hospital.

Along two walls were rectangular tables and chairs to match. An older man and his wheelchair-bound wife sat across from each other, sharing a meal together. In two opposite corners, couches and easy chairs were set at an angle to television sets. One carried a sports channel, while the other was tuned to a soap opera.

It was as homey-feeling as a room in a hospital could get. There were colorful rugs on the floor and frilly lace curtains on the windows. Even so, there was no denying that the atmosphere still felt oppressed.

"This is where patients and their families hang out together," he explained as he moved toward a wheelchair-bound, glaring, surly teenaged boy. The young man's parents were seated on a sofa next to him, and Vince sympathized with the expressions on their faces. They looked like they might be at the end of their rope, trying to communicate with him. It was bad enough for any parent to try to communicate with their teenager. With what the boy had been through, it was a million times worse.

Vince knew the Andersons well. They'd been staying at Morningway Lodge for a month now, but had made little progress with their son, Justin.

Justin didn't want to acknowledge the snowboarding accident that had left him paralyzed.

He didn't want to be in the hospital. Most days, he didn't want to be alive at all.

Vince knew from his years at the lodge, praying with hospital residents and their families, that many patients went through such stages and eventually worked through the feeling that their lives were over. He prayed Justin would find that peace as well. And for his parents' sake, soon.

"There's not a lot of room here," Melanie commented. "For as many people as are using the facility, I mean."

"The grounds are beautiful in the summertime," he said. "And there are an abundance of walkways specially made for wheelchairs. Of course, that doesn't help in wintertime."

He smiled down at her. "All this to say that, yes, I agree with you. There's not much privacy here. The hospital board is working on it, though. Another dayroom is being added this spring to accommodate all the extra patients they've got coming in."

He paused and frowned as he mentally adjusted to the weight of stress that came slamming back down on his shoulders, along with a sudden sharp throbbing in his temple that warned of the beginning of a headache he was all too familiar with.

"Morningway Lodge should be expanding as well," he continued gruffly. "But I don't even know how we're going to rebuild the day care."

Melanie turned a concerned gaze on him, but he brushed it off with a shrug even though his own worries didn't dissipate nearly as easily as he would have liked her to think they did.

This was his problem, not hers. The last thing he wanted Melanie to see was his apparent lack of faith in God to work all things for the good. Deep in his heart he knew he believed God would work things out, even if he didn't feel that way right now emotionally.

He turned his attention to the people in the dayroom, hoping Melanie didn't notice how tense he was. He gestured her forward and they toured the room, speaking with everyone they passed as they went.

Fortunately, Melanie didn't possess even an ounce of the reserve that Vince was cursed with, and she made instant friends of the patients and their families, except perhaps Justin, who thought he didn't need or want a friend.

Given time, though, Vince was certain even Justin would warm to Melanie. She had a way about her that brought smiles to all those she came in contact with, and her energy was as infectious as her smile.

Just what these patients needed. Just what Vince could not do for them.

And just as impossible as plucking a star from the sky, the idea of him and Melanie working together. Ministering together both here and at the lodge. What a far-fetched daydream that was. Yet how could he help but think of it?

Her strengths were his weaknesses, which was why, he supposed, Nate had hired her in the first place. Because she really could— *did*—help him.

Melanie clearly cared about the people she came in contact with here at the hospital, and he had to continually remind himself that this was a one-time shot. She was only here in the first place because he'd coerced her into it. She was a businesswoman, and her life was far away from Morningway Lodge. She was here to do a project at the lodge, and then she'd be gone.

Gone.

He shook his head, clearing his thoughts. No

use dwelling on the impossible. God had yet to do His work on Melanie's heart; and even then, she'd still be leaving.

He glanced at his wristwatch. They were already twenty minutes late getting back to Pop, and Vince knew he was going to hear about it later. Pop would pitch a fit, although not until Melanie was no longer present.

But surprising even himself, the always-dependable and always-on-time Vince Morningway didn't care if he was late. It was worth every second to be with Melanie, and he didn't regret a moment of it.

Except maybe how this visit might be affecting Melanie, which was still a concern. He would never want to hurt her, even unintentionally.

As they walked back to the physical therapy gym, an uncomfortable silence loomed over them. At least it was uncomfortable for Vince.

Melanie wasn't talking. And for once, he really wished she would.

Oh, wow. Melanie leaned her arms against the sink in the small bathroom connected to her room at the lodge. She stared disparagingly at her reflection in the mirror.

What in the *world* had she done?

She watched as the unfortunate scarlet color crept up her neck, over her cheeks and then all the way up to her forehead. Blushing made her clash with her own self.

Kissing Vince made her wonder if she'd completely lost her hold on things.

That man brought out so many emotions in her that she couldn't even list them, much less analyze them. Unnamed and uncomfortable feelings dizzily swirled around and around in her heart and head.

She wasn't used to things she couldn't put into order, and it grated against her like a metal rake against a cement sidewalk that she'd somehow lost control of herself around Vince.

She forced herself to breathe in and out slowly.

She could handle this. She *would* handle this.

She hadn't had a real, committed relationship with a man since, well, ever. The abusive relationship between her stepdad and her mother was enough to convince Melanie that a happy marriage was nothing but a myth, and having a family was a bad, *bad* idea.

Consequently, every time a man showed any real attraction to her, she'd draw back both physically and emotionally until he lost interest. No matter how hard she tried, she just couldn't commit. She wasn't a runaway bride; she was a runaway first date.

In her defense, she'd never experienced a kiss with the fierce, fiery impact made between her and Vince—the instant connection, the sparkling electricity and the feeling, just for a moment, that it was something special. That she meant something to him.

Which made less than no sense because she'd instigated the kiss—short, sweet and over before it started.

And now she had to go and face him and pretend nothing had happened between them. This was, in a sense, new ground she was breaking; yet in some ways it felt all too familiar.

She was good at pretending. Pretending her real father had not abandoned her and her mother when she was born. Pretending she hadn't hid under the bed as a child to avoid her violent and abusive stepfather, who spat fire-and-brimstone Bible verses at her and her mother while threatening to beat them up for their sins.

The easiest route, she recognized, was simply to walk away from this new situation, which frightened her in a completely different way, elevating her emotions rather than deflating them.

The business project was keeping her here, but she knew it was so much more than that. A business project she could walk away from if she had to. She wasn't certain she could walk away from Vince. There was the softest whisper in her ear suggesting that *no, with Vince, this time was different.*

This *man* was different.

Different from her stepfather. Different than any of the men she'd dated in the past—big-city businessmen whose main goals in life were wealth and status.

She'd thought she was one of them. Now she wasn't so sure. She liked the peacefulness and grandeur of life in the Rocky Mountains.

She pulled on her hiking boots. They felt more natural on her feet now that she'd been wearing them awhile—no more blisters. In fact, she would have to say they were actually *com-*

fortable, much like the old, faded blue jeans she was wearing. Who would have thought?

She grabbed her attaché and was halfway out the door when she remembered she had somewhere else she needed to go besides Vince's office, before the inevitable first-time-after-kissing encounter with him.

She recalled that she wanted to find Nate and talk to him about helping out with whatever scheme the man had hatched for Vince.

The weather was moderate for this time of year—no recent snowstorms and no wind to bump up the chill factor—and she found Nate swinging baby Gracie in one of those chair swings designed especially for toddlers. Gracie was all bundled up in her pink snowsuit, but Nate wore only an unzipped black bomber jacket over his olive green T-shirt.

Melanie, herself dressed as warmly as possible, in a heavily lined stylish parka over a thick sweater, thought the man must be nuts.

For a moment, she reconsidered what she was about to do. Though she didn't yet know all the particulars, she knew Vince didn't get along with Nate. There was a lot of bad blood there, and Nate was potentially stirring the pot by doing whatever he was planning on doing behind Vince's back.

And she was seriously considering aiding him?

But Nate had said it was a surprise, so presumably that was a good thing. And if it *was* something that would help Vince out, Melanie wanted to be a part of it.

Nate noticed her approach and waved at her just as she was about to call out to him. Jessica, dressed in a sweat suit, was seated at the bottom of a nearby slide and stood to greet her as Melanie approached.

She stopped before Nate and smiled at the baby, who was waving her arms and exclaiming in delight.

"I want to help you with your surprise for Vince," Melanie blurted out without preamble and before she lost her nerve.

Nate's face lit up and his smile widened. "I can't tell you how glad I am to hear that."

Jessica gave Melanie a spontaneous hug, which surprised her as much as it cheered her.

"Welcome aboard," Jessica said enthusiastically.

Melanie hadn't been given even the smallest

of details about whatever plan Nate and Jessica had concocted, but for the oddest reason, she *did* feel welcome into their little family, a coconspirator in keeping their big secret.

Whatever that was.

"We can't wait to tell you about it," Jessica said enthusiastically.

Melanie chuckled. To their credit, Nate and Jessica seemed to be genuinely nice people who readily opened their hearts to newcomers like Melanie. Yet for some reason Vince didn't feel nearly as amicable to Nate as one would think he would be, and she knew him well enough to know he must have his reasons. He and Nate were brothers, and Melanie had seen for herself how softhearted Vince was under that gruff exterior.

So what was she missing? What was it about Nate that Vince found so frustrating and infuriating?

Melanie brushed the question aside and chuckled. "I'm happy to help, but I'd like to know exactly what it is you two are up to."

"We *three*," Nate corrected, nodding his head toward Gracie, who was now wailing and wiggling in an attempt to get herself out of the constricting swing. He pulled the baby into his arms and gave her a smacking kiss on her button nose. "Gracie loves her uncle Vince and wants him to be happy, don't you, sweetheart?"

"And this would happen *how?*" Melanie asked, wondering how Nate could be so easy-going when his brother always took things too seriously.

"Oh," Nate enthused. "The *plan!*" He swung Gracie around and made her giggle.

Jessica smiled indulgently at her fiancé. "What Nate means to say—and may never actually get to as long as he has Gracie here to distract him—is that we are planning a fundraising event at the lodge to make enough money to rebuild the daycare."

Melanie's heart jolted to life. Whatever qualms she may have had about conspiring with Nate instantly vanished like mist in the morning sunshine.

This was exactly what Vince needed!

"Tell me more," she pleaded, knowing her excitement was bursting through in her voice.

"We've lined up quite a number of guests. Some are past donors to Morningway Lodge. We've got the requisite corporate philanthropists. But mostly they are people who've stayed here at the lodge in the past and now want to give back. We have quite a few guests who have indicated an interest in getting up to speak to the group to express their gratitude to Vince for being there when they needed him."

Melanie's heart welled into her throat, and she fought back tears of emotion. Nate and Jessica had once had their names in the newspaper for rescuing those kids from the fire at the day care, and it was well-deserved.

But Vince? He was the unsung hero, privately laboring to minister to those in need without expecting any kudos for his work.

Finally, he would be able to see just how much he meant to the people he'd helped.

To Nate and Jessica.

To her.

"I'm in," she assured them, wrapping her arm around one of the posts on the swing set and leaning her shoulder into it. The metal was freezing cold but she didn't care. "However, I'm not at all clear about what exactly it is you want me to do. It sounds like you guys pretty much have everything under control without me."

"We still have to set up catering and work out the logistics," Nate said.

"Sure," Melanie replied. "I could help with that."

"We would appreciate any help you can give us. However, what we need *you* to do is keep Vince…" Jessica paused, a sly grin spreading across her face "…occupied. You know, distracted a little bit."

Don't blush, don't blush, don't blush, Melanie coaxed herself, but she felt the heat rising to her face despite her best efforts.

"How?" she asked, trying not to let her mind conjure the romantic scene Jessica was probably thinking of, judging by the way her lips were twitching. Melanie knew it would only stain her cheeks from pink to a dark red that surpassed even her hair color.

"Mostly we just need you to do what you're already doing," Nate said, apparently completely unaware of his fiancée's double meaning. "Keep him busy in the office—not like that isn't where Vince spends all his time anyway," Nate said, his lips twisted sardonically.

"I can do that," Melanie assured him.

"Yeah, that shouldn't be a problem. But there is one more thing."

Melanie quirked an eyebrow.

"On the actual day of the fundraiser, we need

to get him off the grounds completely, so that we can bring the guests in without him seeing anything," Jessica added, moving to Nate's side and brushing her hand softly down over his arm. It was a comfortable, tender gesture, a genuinely loving moment between a soon-to-be happily married couple, and something with which Melanie was completely unfamiliar.

"I have no idea how I'm going to do that," Melanie admitted with a shrug, but then she squared her shoulders, determination winning out over fear—at least for now.

"Oh, I don't know," Jessica teased, drawing out the words and winking at Melanie, as if they shared a private joke, woman to woman. "I've been working with Vince for over a year, and I've never seen his eyes light up the way they do when he is around you. I'm sure you'll think of *something*."

Chapter Eleven

"I don't get it," Vince announced, and he wasn't just talking about the computer spreadsheet he had opened before him on his laptop computer, as annoying as that might be. The program, while problematic, wasn't nearly as confusing as the mixed signals he was getting from Melanie. He still wasn't sure what had happened between them—or rather, what *hadn't* happened between them.

Nearly a week had gone by since he'd taken her to the hospital with him. Nearly a week since they'd kissed, and they hadn't talked about it or even acknowledged it.

The curser blinked in rhythm, reminding him that he should be concentrating on the data Melanie was entering, but how could a man think when his senses were overwhelmed by the citrus scent of her shampoo? He was trying to ignore the way her presence unnerved him, but that wasn't so easy to do.

He supposed he expected Melanie to bring up the subject. Surely she would want to talk about it. She was always perfectly straightforward with him, and she had an opinion on everything else in his life. Why not this, which seemed so monumentally important as compared to what color of file folders he chose to use. But she acted as if nothing had happened between them, and he didn't know what to say, so he didn't say anything.

That's not to say he didn't think about it, though—a lot, actually. Late at night, when he was lying in bed and couldn't seem to get his brain to turn off. Every morning, when he prayed for her. And especially now, when he was leaning over her—ostensibly to point at the computer screen, but in truth, just wanting to be near her.

Red hair and freckles could be the downfall of a man.

Melanie whirled around in the office chair, surprising Vince and catching him off guard as she stood. He would have taken a step backward, except that his blooming leg cast would have caused him to take a digger.

"You," she accused, poking a finger in his chest, "are not paying attention." She stared up at him, daring him to deny it, which of course he couldn't do.

Oh, he was paying attention, all right. Just not to the stupid computer spreadsheet, which he couldn't care less about anyway.

"What's that smile for?" she demanded.

He immediately voided his expression, even though he felt a little like laughing at the way she cocked her head and perched her hands on her hips.

Laughing! What was happening to him?

"What smile?" he asked innocently.

She ignored his question and asked one of her own. "What were you thinking about just now?"

His gaze flickered to the laptop, and he briefly considered lying to her, giving her the answer she no doubt expected to hear. Instead, he reached out his hand and threaded his fingers with hers.

"You."

There was a flash of vulnerability in her eyes

as she absorbed what he had just said to her, but she didn't look away from him.

"I want to kiss you again." He'd always been too blunt when he spoke, and now was no exception. He was pretty positive he shouldn't have phrased his intentions quite that way. Probably, he should have just kissed her.

"You didn't kiss me, I kissed you," she reminded him, surprising him with her tart response.

Her chin tilted upward just the littlest bit, inviting him to make good on his declaration.

He wasn't going to give her the opportunity to change her mind. He dropped his cane, not caring about the racket it made when it hit the floor. His grip slid from her fingers to her waist as he pulled her close, cradling the nape of her neck with his other hand, enjoying the soft feel of her hair cascading over the back of his wrist.

He loved her red hair. He loved her freckles. But most of all, he loved the generous, kind person he knew her to be. He was captivated by her, and he was falling hard.

He bent his head and kissed her cheeks and her nose. Those little freckles of hers needed attention. Then he bent a little further and captured her mouth with his, testing his own feelings. And hers.

"You are the sweetest thing ever to come across this mountain," he whispered against her lips.

"You think I'm sweet?" She sounded surprised.

"Hasn't anyone ever told you that before?" He would have thought she had men lined up outside her apartment in Boulder, men with fancy cars and big bouquets of flowers, all hoping to be the lucky guy she chose for her next date.

He knew he wasn't the kind of man a woman like Melanie would usually go for, but if those guys weren't telling her how special she was, he was going to make up for it now.

"No. No one's ever said that to me before," she replied in a hushed tone. She bent back from him just enough for him to see that her big copper-penny eyes were glimmering with moisture. One solitary tear escaped and slowly trickled down her cheek.

His heart jammed in his throat. He hadn't meant to make her cry. He framed her face with his hands and then kissed away that errant tear.

He didn't stop there, but trailed kisses from her forehead to her jaw.

"You are sweet," he said, punctuating each word with a kiss. "And special. And beautiful."

He had reached her lips again and decided he wanted to spend more time there—a lot more time.

"Oh-I'm-so-sorry-I-didn't-realize-oh-dear-I'll-come-back-later." It sounded like one long, drawn-out word; it had all been said in one breath, and the female voice was definitely coming from the vicinity of the office door.

"Jessica," Vince said, masking the surprise in his voice as he turned toward her, wobbling a little bit on his one good foot before he gained his balance. He would have kept Melanie in his grasp, but she had slipped underneath his arm and, as near as he could tell, was attempting to make herself look invisible behind his back.

"Not looking!" Jessica had her hand cupped over her eyes, but it didn't cover her delighted smile.

"It's okay," Vince assured her.

"Vince. *Melanie*." Jessica chuckled as she emphasized Melanie's name. "Again, so sorry. I just came by, Vince, because you'd left a number of messages on Nate's cell and I wanted to make sure they were nothing urgent."

"I see. And why isn't Nate here instead of you?" Vince asked, feeling the old, familiar pull of tension returning to his neck.

"I'm afraid he's away on business," Jessica explained with a tentative smile. "Anything I can do for you?"

He shook his head to decline Jessica's offer, as well-intentioned as it might have been. There wasn't anything urgent about any of his phone calls. He'd just wanted to check up on Nate—and now, it appeared, with good reason.

"What business?" he asked, not caring if his voice sounded strained. "He didn't say anything to me about having to go anywhere."

"I'm afraid I really couldn't say."

Vince clenched his fists to control his temper, and only took a breath when he felt Melanie's hand resting on his shoulder blade. Nate had *promised* to be available at the lodge while Vince was learning this new computer system. Instead, he'd skipped out without saying a word.

He should have known he couldn't trust his brother with that kind of responsibility. Nate had been neglectful of his chores as a kid.

Clearly he was equally lax with the job he was supposed to do now.

Vince didn't know why he'd expected Nate to change just because he had a fiancée and a baby. Once irresponsible, always irresponsible—at least as far as Nate was concerned. Only now, his reckless behavior was affecting the lodge, and Vince couldn't just let that drop.

"No wonder he won't return my phone calls," Vince grumbled, his voice low. "It appears Nate has gone back to being the immature, careless guy he's always been. Or maybe he never changed at all."

Melanie cringed inwardly and dropped her hand from Vince's back so that he wouldn't feel her shaking. Jessica hadn't lied when she'd told Vince she really couldn't say where Nate was at the moment.

She really *couldn't say*. Not if they were going to keep the fundraiser a surprise. Nate wasn't shirking off his responsibilities—he was in Boulder arranging catering for the big day.

And now Nate would be in a heap of trouble when he returned, and neither one of the ladies could say a word to get him out of it. As the full realization of the situation hit her, Melanie's gut clenched and turned as if her lunch wasn't agreeing with her.

This was all her fault!

She felt a staggering wave of fear and panic, like she was trying to breathe underwater and didn't know how to swim to get to the surface.

She had to *do* something to defuse the impending disaster that was brewing.

Now.

She was supposed to have kept Vince so distracted and otherwise occupied that he wouldn't notice Nate's movements in and out of the lodge. She'd thought she'd succeeded, what with introducing him to his new—and very much improved—computerized financial system. Between that and, er, other things, she'd really, *really* thought she had Vince's full and absolute attention.

She'd obviously thought wrong.

She should have known Vince wouldn't entirely give up the responsibility of running the lodge over to Nate, and not keep his hands in it in some way or another. He was too possessive of, and maybe even obsessed with, the lodge.

Plus, he didn't trust Nate.

Duh! Why hadn't she managed to add it all together before now? What an idiot she was.

There was a single moment—one that Melanie was not proud of—where part of her wanted to shift the blame onto Jessica's shoulders. If Jessica hadn't brought up Nate's lack of response to Vince's phone messages, he wouldn't have realized Nate was gone.

But what if there had been something urgent or even an emergency? Jessica had been right to follow up with him.

Not her fault.

Melanie met Jessica's gaze, silently pleading for help in finding a way out of this mess, but Jessica just smiled and nodded, as if she had full assurance that Melanie could handle this catastrophe.

Jessica seemed to be taking Vince's attitude completely in stride, although Melanie couldn't imagine how. Even if Vince had been *right* in what he was saying about Nate, he was being his old, pigheaded self again. Talk about reverting to old ways. The fact that he was completely and utterly wrong about the situation, albeit unknowingly, just made it worse.

"I'll let Nate know to come see you when he returns," Jessica said, and made a quick exit.

Melanie didn't blame her. She wasn't sure she wanted to be around Vince herself even if, mere minutes before, she had been as happy as she'd ever been—in his arms, and couldn't imagine anywhere else she would ever want to be.

As soon as Jessica was out of earshot, Vince pounded a fist against his desk, groaning as he slid into the office chair. After a moment, he jammed his fingers through his already-spiked hair and sighed loudly.

"I should have known," he said wearily. "I knew I couldn't trust Nate, but I did anyway. It's my own fault for trying to be nice."

Melanie shook her head. If there was any failure here, it was hers. She was supposed to have kept Vince occupied so he wouldn't notice Nate's absence.

Maybe once Vince cooled down, he would be more reasonable about the subject.

"I know I haven't been around all that long, but from everything I've seen, Nate has been faithfully working around the lodge. I believe he was the one who revarnished the front porch, and I think I've seen him digging out some rough spots on one of the mountain trails," she offered.

"Digging up trouble more like," Vince sniped. "Look, Melanie. You're entitled to your opinion about Nate, but you don't really know him. His being a Marine—and now a father—fools people. He was an irresponsible child, always disappearing when there was work to be done. He was reckless and careless, not only with himself, but with other people. The way I see it, he's doing the same thing now."

"Then you see it wrong."

So much for being reasonable—for either of them.

Melanie forgot about her guilt. She was full-out furious with this bullheaded man. Didn't he believe anyone could change for the better?

Vince's expression changed from shocked, to hurt, to downright fuming, all in a matter of seconds. His brow rose well over the top rim of his glasses, then furrowed over his nose before becoming a straight, rigid line. His usually bright blue-eyed gaze became daggers of icicles.

"Stop," he said, his voice so low and gravelly that she could barely understand the words. "Please don't say any more."

Melanie pressed her hands to the desk and leaned over, glaring back at him. "You stop."

She knew she sounded childish. They both did. But that didn't stop her from continuing.

"Cut Nate a break. Why don't you give him the benefit of the doubt for a change. You're not boys anymore. You're a man. Act like one."

Of course, Melanie had had the last word. And then, all the flaming, furious five feet two inches of her stormed out of his office like a regular Irish dervish.

Vince leaned back in his office chair and took off his glasses. With a sigh, he pinched the bridge of his nose where a jagged-edged headache was starting.

He was still angry with Nate, but it was nothing compared to the other emotions that were pulling his brain and heart in a bazillion different directions.

He took a deep, calming breath, determined to regain his focus. He'd never been the kind of man who was ruled by his emotions, and he wasn't going to start now. His strength was in his ability to stay calm and be reasonable. Practical.

Sensible.

There was only one problem—Melanie.

She forced him to face all the things he kept crammed deep inside of him, both good and bad. He was more his true self with her than he'd ever been with anyone. She knew him wholly, and because of that, the sharp words she'd flung at him hit their mark dead-on.

Right through his heart.

It was downright painful. He was ashamed of the way he had acted—or more accurately, *overreacted,* just now. There was no good reason for him to have gone off on her the way he had, except for a ridiculous and completely irrational sense of betrayal when Melanie had stood up for Nate.

Nate, again.

Why did everyone always take it easy on Nate? Why did they take his side in an argument no matter what it was about or who was at fault?

Why couldn't anyone—*Melanie*—understand *his* side of the story for once?

He sighed and reached for the top drawer of his desk where he pulled out a well-worn study Bible. He couldn't control what Nate did or didn't do, or what Melanie thought of him, but getting a grip on his own heart and actions was another thing entirely.

If Nate was the prodigal son, then he, Vince, was the prodigal's older brother—having everything and not even knowing it.

He had really blown it. He cared for Melanie deeply, and this was how he had shown it. What must she think of him?

He had wanted to share his faith with her, but instead he'd trampled on it, right in front of her. The most important thing he could show her was the goodness and mercy of God, the tender love of a Savior who cared.

All he'd managed to do was show her what a mess *he* was. A bad-tempered, ill-mannered lout.

She had already balked at the mere mention of God. Now she was going to hightail it in another direction, spiritually speaking, for sure, all thanks to him.

Unless he did something radical and practically unheard of, like saying he was sorry. He knew it was time for him to man up and apologize for his mistakes, but only God could make it right.

He opened his Bible and turned to the book of Matthew. Getting his focus back on God with prayer and praise was clearly the first thing he needed to do. And since he'd thought of it, he might as well read the story of the prodigal son. Maybe he could learn something from it. After that, he would have to go find Melanie and eat humble pie.

Chapter Twelve

If there had ever been a better display of the proverbial red-headed woman's temper, Melanie didn't know what it was. She had stomped out of his office like a toddler in her terrible twos.

She was *right*, of course, but there had to be a better way to express herself. How unfortunate that her mouth had claimed the better part of her good sense.

Lovely.

Not knowing what else to do and feeling very much at loose ends, she'd returned to her room. But now she was feeling claustrophobic in the small space.

She opened the window. The fresh, freezing cold air hit her right in the face and inside her lungs, and she gasped, welcoming the stinging pain.

The most infuriating thing about the whole situation wasn't even how Vince was acting. She could understand that, even if she didn't agree with it.

What really frightened her was that through it all, even their most temperamental disagreements, her feelings for Vince hadn't changed.

She wasn't scared off by him, even when he was at his angriest. She wasn't *afraid*. Somewhere, somehow, in these weeks with Vince, something fundamental had changed in her heart.

Any other man, any other situation, and her feathers wouldn't have been ruffled. She would have flat-out flown the coop.

But not with Vince.

She must be crazy. Or in love.

And she wasn't crazy.

She tested her feelings for a moment, poking at them to see if they'd explode. They billowed. They welled. But it was a warm, giddy feeling and not a sense of panic that enveloped her heart.

She was in love with Vince.

She sat down on the side of the bed, stunned

by the sudden revelation and feeling inexplicably weak in the knees. What in the world was she supposed to do now?

Most likely, Vince wouldn't even be talking to her at the moment because he considered her as having taken his brother's side of things. And even if he was speaking to her, what would she say to him?

Now that her own anger had been tempered and she'd had the chance to cool off, she could—kind of—see Vince's side of the story.

She had the deep, unnerving premonition, like an ice cube running down her spine, that Nate's big surprise wasn't the best way to earn Vince's trust. The whole plan might well backfire on all of them; and there Melanie was, right in the middle of it. She was just as guilty of keeping secrets as his brother was—and not only that, but on his brother's behalf.

Vince was a proud man, one who might very well resent interference in his business for any reason, even a good one. Especially from Nate and company.

What if he didn't want her around anymore, once this whole shenanigan was over?

She rolled to her stomach facing the edge

of the bed, crossed her feet at the ankles and propped her chin on her hands. She hadn't really given much thought past the end of the six weeks, when she'd be done with her work at the lodge, but she knew one thing for certain: She couldn't just walk away from here—from Vince—and not look back, a job well-done and her promotion in her pocket.

Somewhere along the way, her relationship with Vince had completely superseded her career plans. To her own shock, she didn't really care.

Through Vince's eyes, she'd grown to love Morningway Lodge and the people he served here. There must be some way to make a successful compromise, for love's sake.

For love's sake? She was getting completely carried away.

While she lay there planning her future with Vince, he was mad at her. Might continue to be mad at her. And even if he didn't stay angry, there was still the fact that she had absolutely no idea how he felt about her. Just because she was in love with him didn't necessarily mean he reciprocated her feelings.

He was a confirmed bachelor if she'd ever

seen one. Why would he change his whole life just to be with her?

She had more unanswered questions than she had answers, and she was afraid even to hope.

She was so deep in her thoughts that she jumped right off the bed when someone knocked on her door. Smoothing down her hair and placing a hand on her startled, racing heart, she stepped to the door.

She thought it might be Jessica coming to talk about what had happened with Vince that afternoon and plan a new strategy with her. Melanie definitely knew she could use a little commiseration at the moment, so she enthusiastically opened the door.

"Vince!" she exclaimed, her heart jumping out of the gate like a horse at a rodeo. Given the circumstances, he was the last person on earth she expected to find at her door right now.

His expression grim, he was leaning hard on his cane with one hand. His other hand was poised in a fist at the door to knock again.

"We need to talk." He scrubbed his free hand through his hair and stepped forward, closing the distance between them. His gaze caught hers, his bright blue eyes dilated and dark, and narrowed under his scowl.

Oh boy. Apparently this argument of theirs wasn't over yet, though she could not imagine what he had to say that hadn't already been said, or that would warrant an out-of-the-way visit to her room.

With a sigh, she stepped aside and gestured him inside, then followed him into the room.

"Look, if you're here to—" she started but he cut her off, stopping her with a wave of his hand, like a policeman directing traffic.

"No, that's not it. Just listen."

Whatever it was he wanted to tell her, he was clearly still good and angry. His brow was low, his shoulders were set, and his frown was deep and tight. Melanie thought if the proverbial steam could be billowing out his ears, it would be.

"Take a seat?" she offered, pointing to the one and only chair, made of knotted pine.

Vince glanced behind him and then rubbed the thigh of his hurt leg and grimaced.

"Thanks," he said gruffly.

"No problem." She perched herself on the corner of the bed and wrapped her arms around her knees. She knew it was an instinctively defensive gesture, what with her study of personality and expression, but it was what it was.

Shield up. Armed and ready to deflect whatever irrational, sharp and painful arrows she anticipated would now be shot in her direction.

Vince's frown deepened. His forearms were resting on his knees and his hands were clasped tightly together. For a moment he looked away from her, staring intently at his fists.

If she were to guess, she'd think he was praying. Which was odd. And somehow touching.

His head jerked up. "I'm sorry."

"Come again?" she asked, completely taken off guard by his blunt admission.

"I said I'm sorry." His lips twisted in a half smile. "You aren't one of those women who will make me say it over and over again before I'm forgiven, are you?"

"What? N-no, of course not," she stammered. "You just surprised me, is all."

He scoffed. "Sometimes I surprise myself," he said gruffly. "About how mean and petty I can be, especially when I get my back up. Whatever. I just wanted to tell you that I know

I'm not doing what God wants me to do when I get all snarky like that. I say I'm a Christian and then I don't act like one."

Melanie sat quietly, absorbing what he'd just told her.

Had he been angry? Sure he had.

Did he make mistakes? Plenty. Hadn't they all?

But Vince Morningway had the most genuinely sincere faith in God she'd ever seen. She'd seen it in action enough times to know. He believed with all his heart that Jesus was real. He had a living, personal relationship with God that was so poignant that it even touched Melanie's cold heart—enough for her to be reconsidering what she believed, or rather what she *didn't* believe, about God.

Vince's being here right now, apologizing to her without even trying to shift any of the blame elsewhere, was even more proof that he was a true Christian.

"Melanie?" Vince said when she didn't respond. "Say something. If you're still mad at me, I understand. I'll back off if you want me to. I just wanted you to know that I regret the way I acted today."

Melanie shook her head. "We both lost our

tempers. It happens. Don't beat yourself up about it."

Vince smiled tightly, but it didn't quite reach his eyes. "Thank you."

She uncurled her legs and stood, reaching for his hands, which were still clenched together so tightly that his knuckles were turning white. Gently, she worked them loose.

"I forgive you already. I'm sorry, too. You're off the hook, so relax."

He groaned. "Not quite yet."

"Because...?"

"I caught Jessica in the hallway, and then I came here to talk to you. I've got to make things right with Nate. It's way overdue."

"Really? I wouldn't think that would matter. He's family. It's not the first time you've tussled, and I'm sure it won't be the last. You're brothers. That's what brothers do."

"Yeah, but still," Vince disputed. "This thing between Nate and me has been going on since we were kids. It's not just sibling rivalry, although I wish it were."

Melanie pulled on his hands. "Come on. Come over here and sit beside me." She gestured to the tiny two-seated sofa against the far wall, facing an even smaller television which Melanie had never used.

A loveseat.

"Nate was wrong when he left you with full responsibility of the lodge," she said softly, trying to convey that she understood at least part of what he was going through.

Vince stared at her thoughtfully, his blue eyes soft, but he didn't speak.

"And then when your father suffered a stroke, that put you in the position of running the whole lodge yourself or seeing it fall apart, leaving all those families without many options. It must have been tough on you, but you did it, even as young as you were. You should be proud of yourself."

Vince shook his head. "Don't overglorify what I did. I'm not perfect. I just did what I had to do."

"Nate had the opportunity to make choices with his life that you didn't have." She was only now beginning to see the whole picture, how certain events had molded his life, making him into the man he was now.

He was silent, his mouth pursing as he stared down at their interlaced hands. He stroked his thumb across hers in a methodical rhythm.

She squeezed his hand. "If Nate hadn't left and your father hadn't suffered a stroke, what would you have done differently? Where do you see yourself being now?"

Vince's gaze snapped to hers, his blue eyes, luminescent through his glasses, wide with surprise.

"I'd be here."

Chapter Thirteen

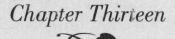

Vince swallowed hard at the sudden, unbidden burning in the back of his throat.

He would be *here*.

Nate hadn't given him a choice, and his father's stroke couldn't possibly have been anticipated. Just as he'd told Melanie, at the time it had all happened, he'd simply done what he'd had to do.

But even if Nate hadn't left, and Pop hadn't had a stroke, Vince would still be here at Morningway Lodge, laboring to help others. All his life, he'd watched his father's ministry at the lodge, and he'd known that someday the family business would be his—his and Nate's.

And he'd *wanted* it that way.

He'd never really seriously considered doing anything else with his life. He now realized he had been angry with Nate because, ironically, he'd always imagined sharing the ministry with his brother, and not because he couldn't be the one who left the lodge to pursue a different career.

He turned a little bit toward Melanie, until their knees were touching, and cleared his throat. "You know you've just knocked an entire decade of preconceived notions right out the window?"

Her right eyebrow twitched up and she grinned wickedly. "Didn't I mention I'm really good at that? I'm not even going to charge you extra. Consider it part of my job."

"Whatever Nate is paying you, it isn't enough."

"Don't worry," she said, squeezing his hand. "This particular assignment has been well worth my while."

Why did he get the feeling she wasn't talking about the money she was making? Maybe it was the way her copper-penny eyes sparkled with mischief, and something else he couldn't—or was afraid to—define.

"How did you know I was going to answer that way? You could have been opening a major can of worms. I might have gone off and listed a hundred other things that I wanted to be and places where I wanted to go."

Melanie shook her head. "No, you wouldn't. I've seen you at the hospital, remember?"

He remembered. Every detail of every second. Especially their kiss.

"You can't fool me with that gruff exterior, Vincent Morningway. You may be tough on the outside, but inside, you're just a big ol' softie with a heart of gold."

His lips twisted. Just what every man wanted to hear.

She leaned over and kissed his cheek, which only made things worse, as he thought he might have been blushing.

Now, he knew he was. Feeling a bit dazed, he put a hand over his cheek to cover it up, but then realized it looked like he was sealing her kiss.

Maybe, unconsciously, he was.

"I only wish—" he started, and then broke off as abruptly as he'd begun.

"Wish what?" she asked gently.

"Oh, nothing."

He was going to say he wished Nate would have stayed around and helped him run the lodge, instead of running off and joining the

Marines, so it could have been a joint venture between the two brothers and not what Vince now realized had been a lonely few years. But he just couldn't get those words to leave his mouth, not even for Melanie.

Besides, Nate was home now, determined to take his place at the lodge and to make up for lost time. Look how that was going for them.

"Wish what?" she repeated.

"I wish Nate would get his head on straight and really start helping out around here."

That was the farthest thing from what he'd been about to say, but he couldn't take it back. Not without compromising himself even worse—or having to explain what he was really thinking.

The smile had dropped from Melanie's lips and she was looking at him like—what?

Like he was a stubborn idiot?

He would have to agree with that assessment.

He wanted to tell her what was really in his heart, but there was no way he would be able to pull his thoughts together enough to make audible words with them, so he just shrugged and said nothing.

She stared at him for a moment, her gaze

so sharp and piercing that he felt like she was digging right into his mind, searching for answers.

He didn't know what she expected to find. He shrugged again.

"New topic?" she suggested.

He sighed in relief. "Please."

"So," she said, drawing out the word as if they'd simply been engaged in a neutral conversation and not an emotional roller coaster, "When do you get your cast off?"

"A week from tomorrow. Why?"

"Perfect."

"Why?" he asked again, the hair prickling at the back of his neck. She was planning something in that female head of hers. He could just feel it.

He hoped she wasn't concocting some kind of arrangement to bring him and Nate together somehow, which, given their recent conversation, was a logical deduction to make.

Melanie, bless her heart, wanted to fix everything. It was in her blood. But it wouldn't work. Not this time. Not until he was completely ready to face himself, and even though he would like to think such spiritual growth would occur quickly, he knew it wouldn't be overnight.

"You've shown me your world," she said softly, releasing his hand and brushing her palm down his shoulder. "Now I would like to show you a little glimpse of mine."

Melanie pulled her royal-blue Eclipse in front of the lodge and shut off the engine, but she didn't immediately rush inside to get Vince.

Events couldn't have worked out any better if Melanie had tried. The fundraiser was coming along without a single hitch, other than Nate having been caught away from the lodge, and even then, to her knowledge, Vince had assumed nothing out of the ordinary.

Melanie and Jessica had planned and prepared the decorations. Nate had arranged for catering for the event. The guest list was set. The dining area was going to be full to overflowing tonight, after everyone arrived at the lodge, which would be happening throughout the day.

Best of all, Melanie had figured out how to get Vince completely away from the lodge without raising his suspicion in the least. He was due to be in Boulder to get his cast off, and Melanie offered to drive him.

After that, she'd talked him into lunch, which unbeknownst to him, was going to be a huge production in itself. If all went as planned, the two of them wouldn't be returning to the lodge before nightfall, when the fundraiser was set to begin.

And she'd never had this much fun planning a party in her life. Of course, there hadn't been many parties. But still. The anticipation was killing her, despite—or maybe because of—the fact that Vince might not take the *surprise* part of the party in quite the way they all hoped he would.

Now that the day of the fundraiser had arrived, she had a knot in the pit of her stomach the size of Colorado. Her gut clenched even tighter as Vince hobbled toward her, taking his time getting down the front steps of the lodge.

"Your car needs a bath," he commented as he slid into the passenger seat and adjusted his legs so that his cast, barely, fit inside.

"Tell me about it," she answered. "Buckle up."

"Aw, you're no fun. Buckle up in a sports

car? I don't suppose you'll let me drive it on the way back to the lodge?" he asked hopefully, flashing her a pouty, wide-eyed expression that reminded her of a puppy begging for table scraps. Or, more to the point, a teenaged boy begging for the car keys.

She burst out laughing at the very *thought* of Vince not buckling his seat belt when he drove. Sensible, follow-the-rules Vince putting the top down and letting loose?

But then, he'd surprised her at every turn, in more ways than she could count. He wasn't exactly a textbook personality profile.

"What?" he asked, his brow rising.

"Nothing." She was not quite successful in smothering her laugh. "You can drive on the way back if you want to."

"Seriously? You'd trust me with this beauty?"

"I'd trust you with a lot of things." *Like my heart*. She didn't say the words aloud.

He grinned. "Way cool!"

He sounded as excited as a young man during his first time behind the wheel. She smiled again. This was a day for happy things, and it looked like Vince agreed. He leaned back in the seat and grinned at her, looking as relaxed and carefree as she'd ever seen him. Maybe it was the thought of getting the cast off his leg that was working wonders. But whatever it was, Melanie liked it.

"Ready for take-off, Captain," he said. "Why don't you gun it on the back roads and see how fast this baby can go?"

She didn't know how fast her car could go, but she doubted it could catch up to the thrumming of her heart.

"You look good," she commented, putting the car into drive. "I like the tie."

He was dressed in tan slacks and a semi-new-looking dark brown sport coat—much nicer than the one he'd been wearing when they first met. His crisp white shirt looked like it was new right out of the package, and he wore a black silk tie loosely around his neck, having unsecured the top button of his shirt.

"Yeah, about that," he said with a chuckle. "Why did I have to get dressed up again? I don't mind the jacket so much, but I really hate wearing a tie."

"Oh, don't be such a baby. I have a surprise planned for you, and you have to be dressed for it."

He grimaced. "I don't like surprises."

"You're going to like this one," she assured him. That was kind of true. She thought he'd probably enjoy an upscale meal at the private lunch she'd arranged for them.

The fundraiser, not so much.

He'd put a public face on it when the guests were there of course—partly because it was a good cause, the day care, and partly because he didn't like airing his dirty laundry in public.

But afterward?

He might line her and Nate up for the firing squad.

Vince couldn't believe how good it was to stretch his ankle, never mind walking around without the cast, though he still felt unbalanced. He'd gotten used to having the weight on his leg, and now it felt strangely light, almost weightless.

"Are you sure you're okay?" Melanie asked as she signaled, and then pulled the car into the parking garage beneath a contemporary-looking building that was several stories high. Its architecture was all shiny metal and glistening glass. Very high-tech. Very Boulder.

Morningway Lodge must have seemed really old-fashioned and behind-the-times to Melanie, although the only comment she'd ever made in that regard was concerning Vince's financial system.

"Good," he answered, even though he didn't really feel that way. He was feeling a little queasy, if truth be told, but he was positive she was talking about his leg, so his answer wasn't exactly a lie. "I'm fine."

"Maybe you should have brought your cane along."

He straightened, trying to convince Melanie—and himself—that he could walk just fine on his own, thank you very much. Every forward step he took was stronger and easier for him. Kinda.

They entered the elevator and Vince stood catty-corner to her, leaning casually against the rail for support. She was silent and her eyes were focused on the sliding door, but his gaze lingered on her.

Melanie was in her element here, he realized. Perfect hair. Perfect makeup. A stylish dress. Heels so high that they added three inches to her height. Her black attaché case was tucked under one arm. She was the epitome of a perfectly polished businesswoman.

The attaché case was the only thing Vince

recognized from her attire. Even at the lodge, she had carried it everywhere. But at the lodge, she'd been wearing jeans, thick, comfortable sweaters and hiking boots. If he'd had to guess, he would say she hadn't spent nearly as much time with her hair and cosmetics while she was staying with them, looking much more natural and not quite so made up.

And although she'd no doubt disagree, he thought he liked her better that way. Go figure.

"I'll show you my office first, and then I'd like you to meet my boss. You'll like her."

She walked ahead of him through a wide, bustling room full of cubicles. Who could work all boxed up like that?

Him, he realized. He might live in the open air of the mountains, but mostly he holed himself up in his tiny office day in and day out.

As he followed her through the room, Melanie greeted each coworker she passed. Everyone clearly knew her and liked her. No big surprise there.

All around the outside of the room were glass-walled offices. Melanie gestured him into the corner office on the far left.

"This one's mine," she said, but Vince

probably could have guessed that by the meticulous organization he saw there. Even within an administrative building of organizers, her office stood out. The contemporary decor was especially impressive, and he wondered if Melanie might have done it herself.

The only thing that looked out of place in the room was a large pile of pink telephone messages that had been driven down over a spike made for that purpose.

Melanie moved to the far window and, crossing her arms, silently gazed out.

"Will you get a new office along with your new promotion?" he asked.

"Hmm?" she asked as she turned to him. Her gaze was a little bit distant and he sensed that he had interrupted her thoughts.

"Promotion? A new office?" he prompted.

"Oh. No," she said, shaking her head. "I like this one. Come over here and take a look at this view."

He walked over and stood behind her, jamming his hands in his pockets to keep himself from reaching for her. She suddenly seemed way out of his league. He reluctantly shifted his gaze from her to where she was pointing.

It *was* a stunning view of the Rocky Mountain

Front Range, with cliffs and snow-covered peaks.

Still, he'd rather be *in* the mountains than looking at them. Maybe he was as backward as he felt.

"Beautiful, huh?" she asked softly.

His gaze returned to her.

"Yeah," he agreed, but he wasn't talking about the mountain view, as nice as that was.

She turned and smiled at him, and the word *beautiful* echoed over and over in his mind. He'd never met a woman like Melanie before, and he knew he never would again.

Melanie looked over his shoulder and her smile widened.

"Joan!" she exclaimed. "I'd hoped you would be around this afternoon."

Melanie's boss walked straight up to Vince and vigorously shook his hand, her eyes bright with gaiety. "Luckily, yes. And unless I miss my guess, you must be Vincent Morningway."

"Guilty as charged," he said, smiling at Joan and wondering how she would know who he was. He was a little relieved at her easygoing style. He liked her.

The next moment, he thought he may have

been a bit premature in forming an opinion about the gregarious woman.

Joan took one step back, propped her hands on her hips and gave Vince a head-to-toe once-over that had him squirming in his shoes.

"I approve," Joan said with a mischievous smile. She gave Melanie a look Vince couldn't even begin to decipher.

Approve of what?

When he heard Melanie's uncomfortable chuckle from behind him, he decided he didn't even want to know.

"Vince, this is my friend and supervisor, Joan Whittaker. And yes, Joan, this is Vince Morningway."

It seemed a bit late for a formal introduction, but he nodded anyway.

Melanie seemed to be as ill at ease as he was, but Joan didn't seem to notice—or maybe she did and thought the best way to get around any awkwardness was to barrel straight through it.

"Mel, I'm sure you've already noticed that you have a bazillion phone messages. Maggie's last day was over a week ago and it's been a crazy few days here."

Joan glanced at Vince and continued speaking

for his benefit. "Maggie is the previous director of operations—the position Melanie is moving into."

She turned her attention back to Melanie. "Anyway, I've been funneling all of Maggie's old stuff onto your desk. Sorry. You'll have to play a little catch-up when you return to the office."

That, Vince decided, was Joan's long-winded and not-so-subtle way of telling Melanie the promotion was hers. If anyone deserved kudos, it was Melanie. He smiled at Melanie, wanting her to know how happy and proud of her he was that she'd gotten the promotion she'd worked so hard for.

Except deep down, if he were being honest, he wasn't *entirely* happy for her. It was absolutely and totally selfish, but a small part of him wanted Melanie to stay with him, which wouldn't happen after she moved back to Boulder permanently and started working in her new position. He looked at his feet, hoping his hesitance didn't show in his smile.

"I don't mind the extra work," Melanie assured Joan. "I'll get right on it."

Vince's gaze snapped to Melanie, but she

wouldn't look at him. She made it sound like...

"So you're finished at the lodge, then?" Joan asked, obviously having come to the same conclusion Vince had.

"I am," Melanie confirmed, and Vince's heart fell. "I have one thing left to do, but I anticipate I'll be completely finished by tonight. I should be back in the office Monday morning."

"Wonderful!" Joan exclaimed.

Horrible! Vince thought.

Whatever was between him and Melanie, a lot of which was unresolved, was coming to an abrupt end. He was speeding toward a brick wall and he couldn't stop the train.

Chapter Fourteen

Melanie was worried. Well, maybe *worried* was the wrong word.

She was terrified.

Vince hadn't said a word to her about the fact that she was leaving the lodge. She didn't know what she had expected. Some sort of protest at least. Maybe not a declaration of undying love, but the least he could have done was to acknowledge that what they had was the beginning of a relationship—not to mention give her some hint as to whether he wanted to pursue it further.

Maybe he didn't need words. Maybe his silence was telling enough.

And even if he did feel something for her now, he'd still probably go ballistic on her once he found out she'd been a willing accomplice to the fundraiser.

It was a short car ride from her office to her friend Erin Girardi's Italian restaurant, where they would be dining. Erin had graciously offered to close the restaurant for Melanie's sole use. She and Vince would have their privacy in spades.

At the moment, she wasn't sure that was such a great idea.

Vince had been polite to Joan, although Melanie privately thought he was acting a little bit more withdrawn than usual. Not that that in itself was cause for alarm. Joan was an acquired taste. Nearly everyone appeared reserved next to Joan, with her sometimes intimidating boisterousness.

Still, Joan was a master at drawing people out, which was part of the reason she'd risen so far in the company. And Vince was no exception. After a while he was smiling and talking about his ministry at Morningway Lodge.

But now?

Nothing. Not a single word.

At this rate, it was going to be a long, *long* lunch, especially because she was going to have to try holding off their return to the lodge until evening. She tried desperately to think of *something* to say, however inane; but at the moment, she could come up with nothing. Nada. Zilch.

She pulled into the parking lot of Girardi's, shut off the engine and turned toward him.

"What's wrong?" In hindsight, being so forthright might not have been the best way to approach this situation, but there it was.

His brow rose over the line of his glasses. "What are you talking about?"

"Well, there's obviously something bothering you, and I thought it might be better to clear the air before we go in and eat. I want you to enjoy your lunch."

"What makes you think something is bothering me?"

"Little clues. You haven't spoken a word since we left my office. You've pushed your glasses up your nose a handful of times. Am I wrong?"

"I promise I'm going to be a model companion this afternoon." He reached for her hand and smiled at her.

She didn't believe for a moment that there wasn't something bothering him, but all she could think of was how much she was going to miss that smile, and that adorable square, dimpled chin of his.

It wasn't just his smile. She was going to miss *him*.

"So we're good?" she asked.

"Absolutely. Is this my surprise?" He gestured to the restaurant. "Food? That works for me. I'm so hungry my stomach is growling. Rowr," he teased, pawing the air like a tiger.

Melanie knew he was deflecting, but at least he was talking.

They entered the dimly lit restaurant and Erin greeted them at the door, took Melanie's jacket from her and directed them to their seats. Candles flickered at every table, but only one was set with a linen cloth and fine china place settings.

Vince was obviously taking in the ambience, and probably the fact that they were the only patrons present. She could see his confusion, and she smiled inwardly.

At least she could do this for him. He had done so much for her. He'd probably never know just how much. He'd never know that she had been so moved by the faith behind his apology that day in her room that when he'd left, she'd slid to her knees by the bedside and asked Vince's Savior to come into her heart and wash her clean as well. Her entire existence changed in that moment, and she knew she'd never be the same again.

Talking about her personal spiritual life wasn't the sort of thing she would feel comfortable just blurting out. She had hoped the opportunity would arise this afternoon. She was certain he'd want to hear about her new life in Christ, and she had so many questions she wanted to ask him about the changes God had brought about in her heart and life.

And it wasn't only her saving faith in Christ that she wanted to talk to him about. Somewhere in the back of her mind, she'd envisioned this as a romantic moment as well.

She hadn't admitted it even to herself until now, but she'd imagined admitting her feelings to him—breaking the news that she was finished with her work at the lodge but not with him.

And in this fantasy, Vince requited those feelings.

The truth hurt. This was no fantasy. This very real scenario was definitely *not* going down that way.

For one thing, she hadn't imagined that

Vince would find out her project at the lodge was finished in quite the way he had; and she sure hadn't expected him to react in the way he did.

Or rather, *not* react.

At all.

So what now? Once they got to the lodge, Vince would be swept away in the celebration.

Was this goodbye?

"Melanie," Vince whispered, tucking his hand under her elbow. "We're the only ones here."

"Exactly," she said, forcing a smile she didn't feel. "I thought you deserved to celebrate getting that cast off your leg."

"But a restaurant all to ourselves? I have to say I'm impressed."

She shrugged. "I have my resources."

"I guess you do," he said with a low whistle. He reached for her chair and seated her, then sat down opposite her, his palms face down in front of him. "I think we should also celebrate a job well done on your part. I haven't yet congratulated you on your promotion."

"Thank you." Her voice cracked when she said it.

Don't cry. Don't cry. Don't cry.

Her inner coaching wasn't working, and she felt the burn of tears in the back of her eyes, fighting to be free.

Vince tilted his head, looking at her thoughtfully. "Maybe I should be the one asking you what is wrong. Even in this lighting, I can see that you're as white as a sheet."

Melanie shook her head. "No, it's nothing. I just felt a little lightheaded there for a moment."

"Here. Drink this," he offered, pressing a glass of cold water into her hands.

She took a sip of the cold liquid and smiled tentatively. "Thank you. I'm feeling much better now."

It was only a small lie and well-meant. If she wasn't careful, she was going to go and ruin Vince's whole day, and that was the last thing she wanted to do.

He had enough of a shock coming to him with the fundraiser. He didn't need a hysterical woman professing her undying—and unrequited—love, throwing herself at him.

She opened her menu and pretended to study it. In truth, she couldn't even see the words, which had blurred on the page from the unshed tears in her eyes.

And then she realized she was *hiding behind the menu.*

How pathetic. She needed to pull herself together, if not for her own dignity, then at least for Vince's sake.

Swallowing hard, she folded her menu and placed it in front of her. "I highly recommend the vegetable lasagna," she said. "Erin's minestrone soup is phenomenal. And just wait until you taste her breadsticks."

Up until that moment, she'd been gazing at her hands, folded on top of her menu. Then she looked up.

Apparently Vince hadn't yet even consulted his menu; it was still lying flat under the palms of his hands. Instead, his eyes were on her.

"I'll have whatever you're having," he said with a wink. "I trust your taste, except maybe in the colors you selected for my file folders. Fluorescent pink and yellow? Really?"

She couldn't help but chuckle, and a little bit of the black cloud hanging over her lifted. She had this one afternoon to spend with him, just the two of them. She wasn't going to ruin it by sulking.

"Complain all you want to, but you'll always be able to find the information you need."

"I believe you."

Erin came up at that moment with her pad in her hand and took their orders, which ended up being exactly the same, except that Vince ordered extra blue cheese on his salad, and Melanie opted for vinegar and oil on the side.

Erin was a good waitress—not hovering but always there to refill their sodas or clear away empty plates. There were several courses planned at slow, even intervals, and Melanie paced herself while she ate, trying to keep things moving along as slowly as possible.

Despite herself, she started to relax as they ate. Vince was easy for her to talk to, and as long as they stayed on safe subjects, it wasn't too hard for her to pretend she was having a good time, that this wasn't the end. And she might have believed it, too, if it were not for that tiny, imaginary clock in her head, ticking off the seconds until they walked out of the restaurant door and their time together was over.

Permanently.

Their meal finally over, Vince leaned back in his seat and sighed contentedly. He was stuffed after all those courses—an appetizer, soup, a salad, breadsticks, lasagna and melt-in-your-mouth tiramisu for dessert. Melanie was absolutely correct about the food being excellent—it was by far the best Italian food he'd ever eaten.

It's just that there was so *much* of it. They'd probably spent a good two hours at the restaurant already.

Not that Vince minded. As long as he was with Melanie, it didn't matter where he was or what he was doing.

He only hoped he wasn't too slow out of the gate, now that he'd discovered she was finished with her project at the lodge and was planning to return to Boulder. Had he waited too long to say something?

It wasn't until Melanie had made that stark admission that his dawdling head finally caught up to his racing heart. He'd been so incredibly blind that it practically took a bold banner waving from the tail end of an airplane for him to put together what would probably have been blatantly obvious to any other man.

He was in love with Melanie.

Get-down-on-one-knee-and-propose-to-her kind of love, the kind of love that changed a man's whole life in one second. And this was the moment.

Too bad he hadn't known about this romantic venue in advance so that he could have taken advantage of it. Too bad he'd taken so long to figure out his own heart.

So the question was, what did he do now?

He could hardly blurt out *I love you,* much as he wanted to. He liked things straightforward, and although he knew Melanie did, too, he thought that tactic was a bit *too* straightforward. But tiptoeing around this issue might drive him crazy.

"I heard what you told Joan." It was a start anyway, a step in the right direction.

"Which part?" she asked, her right eyebrow arching.

Vince put his elbows on the table and leaned toward her. He was well aware that she knew exactly which part of the conversation he was talking about. She was clearly trying to avoid the subject, but Vince pressed on.

"You said you were finished with your work at the lodge. Is that true?"

"Yes." She looked away from him, somewhere over his left shoulder.

"So you're saying you'll be packing up and heading back home to Boulder tomorrow?"

"Something like that." She pinched her lips and nodded. Her gaze returned to his, but it was as if a metal shield had come down over her eyes.

Melanie was a woman full of every kind of beautiful, symphonic emotion, a woman who could make his heart sing and his spirit soar. But now she was mentally retreating, and he didn't know why.

This was not going well, he thought with a jolt of panic. Why was she closing herself off to him now, shutting him out? Clearly she didn't want to talk about her work being finished; but if they didn't talk about leaving, they couldn't get to the part where he asked her to stay.

He tapped his fingers rhythmically against the tabletop, mentally considering his options. Soft strains of Italian music reached his ears, and he smiled.

Making a snap decision and praying it was the right one, he stood to his feet and shrugged out of his sports coat, laying it across the back of his chair. Slowly and methodically, he rolled his sleeves a quarter way up his arms, loosened his tie, and then reached his hand out to Melanie.

"Dance with me."

If he could get her into his arms, then this declaration-of-love business might go easier for him.

"But—but there's no dance floor," she stammered.

"So? There's nobody watching us, sweetheart. There's plenty of room right here by our table."

"You just got the cast off your leg."

"You can hold me up." His smile widened. Her protests were getting weaker.

"I don't dance."

He chuckled. It was about time he took her out of her comfort zone, as she had done so many times to him when she'd remodeled his whole business structure. In this case, what was good for the *gander* was good for the *goose*.

"I'll lead. Grant you, I haven't had much practice recently, but my mom made Nate and me take lessons when we were kids. She knew—or prayed, anyway—that we would be running Morningway Lodge when we grew up, and the occasional black-tie affair is part of the business. Fundraisers definitely aren't my thing, but—"

Melanie stood up so quickly her chair nearly careened to the floor, interrupting whatever else he might have said to her. Her mouth went slack for a moment, and her eyes took on a deer-trapped-in-the-headlights appear-ance.

Apparently, he'd taken her way, *way* out of her comfort zone, although he couldn't imagine why. It was just a dance. The music was soft and slow. It wasn't like he was asking her to tango or anything.

He frowned. He hadn't meant to pressure her to do something that obviously disconcerted her so much.

"You won't hurt my feelings if you say no," he amended softly.

"Okay, I'll dance with you already." She sounded upset.

She stepped forward, standing rigidly with about a foot separating them, and placed her left hand on his shoulder, with her right hand braced in waltz form. Her brow was furrowed as though she were concentrating ferociously.

"I don't know what to do with my feet."

He chuckled and wrapped both hands around her tiny waist, drawing her close to him. A small sound came from the back of her throat, but it was only a token protest. Reluctantly, she wrapped both arms around his neck and leaned her cheek against his chest. He wondered if she could hear the rapid thundering of his heart.

He bent his chin to the top of her head and swayed gently to the music, inhaling her unique citrus scent. Despite Melanie's worries, she had no trouble following his lead, and his own leg was feeling just fine.

He closed his eyes, enjoying the simple act of holding her in his arms and simultaneously gathering the courage to declare what was in his heart.

Melanie leaned away from him just as he was getting ready to speak. Her gaze met his, and whatever words he was about to say slammed together in his throat like a multi-car accident on the highway. Her smile was soft. Her eyes held an intoxicating mix of warmth and sorrow.

"I'm leaving—"

"You're leaving—" they said at the same time.

"Go ahead," he offered.

She shook her head. "You first."

Fierce emotions overtook Vince. How could

he ever express the depth of his loyalty, his desire to protect and cherish her, how he would do everything in his power to make her happy? How he missed her when she wasn't with him, and how much joy she brought him merely being by his side.

He loved her.

"Ah, Melanie, sweetheart," he whispered.

It was all he could manage to say. He framed her soft, heart-shaped face in his hands and kissed her, pouring all his emotions into showing how he felt.

She froze for a moment and then softened against him, her fingers tunneling gently into his hair as she kissed him back.

"Ahem." Erin discreetly cleared her throat as she approached them. With Melanie's coat draped over her arm, she shifted from one foot to the other, looking awkward and embarrassed for having interrupted them.

Vince raised his head and slid his arm around Melanie's shoulder, happy when she leaned into him. He wasn't sure he could stand on his own. His legs felt like rubber.

"Excuse me," Erin continued. "I didn't mean to interrupt, but I thought you should know there's been a winter storm warning announced for this area. It's snowing like the dickens outside already, and I didn't want you to get stuck here in town and not make it back up to the mountains."

She slid a cryptic glance at Melanie that Vince couldn't decipher.

Melanie stiffened and stepped away from him, reaching for the jacket Erin held out to her. Frustration seethed through him. He wanted—*needed*—a few more minutes with Melanie, to talk with her in private. And really *speak* this time, Lord willing.

But it was clear their moment had passed. Melanie's gaze was a little anxious, presumably about the change in the weather. Vince reached for the sports coat draped over the back of his chair and reluctantly shrugged into it. They thanked Erin for the wonderful meal, and she walked them to the door.

He tried to offer payment, but Erin turned him down flat. Apparently that was something else Melanie had, in her foresight, taken care of. Being a guy, he felt a little uncomfortable letting her pay, but he figured it was just his male ego talking, so he let it go. It was nice for someone to do something this special for him, even if he wasn't completely at ease with it. She must care—just a little.

Whatever imaginary beating he thought his ego might have taken, it was immediately restored to him and then some when she tossed him the keys to the Eclipse.

As they exited the restaurant, snow flurries blew around them, whiting out everything so that they could hardly see a yard in front of them. Melanie shivered and pulled up the hood of her parka, framing her pretty face with faux fur. There was already at least a couple of inches of snow on the ground, and Vince took Melanie's elbow to help her navigate the slick sidewalk with those high heels of hers.

"I hate driving in bad weather," she explained as Vince opened the passenger door and she fished in the backseat for a snow brush.

"I'll do that," he said, taking the brush from her and gesturing to the seat. "You get in and stay warm."

He slid into the driver's seat and started the engine to get the heater warmed up, and then methodically scraped off the windows. Despite the snowstorm, he was looking forward to the opportunity to drive the Eclipse.

Even more, he realized he'd have a forty-five-minute drive up to the lodge—probably more, given the weather. Maybe he could find a way to speak to her then.

Or maybe not.

The drive was perilous from the get-go, made worse by the fact that he was driving a new luxury sports car instead of his old but reliable four-wheel-drive truck. Tight mountain curves were nothing to play with under the best of circumstances. With the snow quickly freezing on the roads and then just as hastily covered with the next layer of snow, it was downright treacherous.

Add to that virtual whiteout conditions and the whole drive was dangerous beyond belief. It wasn't long before he realized it would have been safer to have stayed in Boulder until the storm played out; but at that point, they might as well have continued to the lodge as to have turned back.

No testing the Eclipse's speed today. And there was certainly no time for any sort of intimate conversation. It took every bit of his attention just to keep the car on the road.

Melanie didn't speak at all, but her jaw was tight and her hands were clenched in her lap— enough to convince Vince that she really *didn't* like driving in bad weather, even when riding as a passenger.

He set his own jaw, vowing to himself that nothing would ever hurt Melanie. Not so long as he was around.

He would get her back home safe to the lodge, and then he would somehow, in some way, convince her that she was *home* safe at the lodge.

Whatever it took, he vowed he would do it.

Chapter Fifteen

Melanie breathed a sigh of relief as Vince pulled up in front of the lodge and parked. Colorado wasn't the best place in the world to live if you didn't like snowstorms. Driving around in Boulder was bad enough, but watching Vince navigate slick, delicate mountain curves and trying to ignore the plunging cliffs that were mere feet from the road itself was downright terrifying.

Any other day, any other situation, and Melanie would have offered to have Vince stay the night in the extra bedroom of her condo and wait for the worst of the storm to be over. Her nice, warm, *safe* condo.

It was obviously the most sensible thing to do under the circumstances, and she was surprised that Vince hadn't suggested something similar. But he'd seemed anxious to return to the lodge, which was probably a good thing, since she didn't know how many of the dozens of guests were waiting for him at the fundraiser he knew nothing about. She couldn't imagine trying to persuade him to go if he had wanted to stay, stubborn man that he was, so she was lucky in that at least. She guessed.

No. Not lucky. It was Providence, and she tentatively thanked God for intervening.

At least they'd managed to make it back to the lodge in one piece. Another item to add to the quickly growing list of things she needed to add to her prayer list. She wondered how many of the guests attending might not have made it through the rough weather, or who had chosen not to make the trip at all.

Many of them were coming from out of state and would be staying at the lodge, so hopefully they'd arrived before the worst of the storm hit, and were settling in comfortably. She found herself oddly anxious to make the fundraiser a success, and wondered if Nate and Jessica were feeling the same way.

"This isn't going to be a fun walk in high

heels," Vince warned her as he parked the Eclipse as close to the front of the building as possible and shut off the engine.

She glanced down at her feet and sighed. "Then we'd best just get it over with. My toes are going to freeze right off, and unfortunately, my hiking boots are in my room."

Not, she mentally amended, that Vince's dress shoes would do much better on the snow and ice than her heels were. Hopefully they'd be able to prop each other up and slip slide their way inside.

He got out and walked around the front of the car, opening the door for her. She sighed and grit her teeth, preparing as best she could for the ice-cold adventure awaiting her.

But before she could put a foot into the snow, he easily scooped her into his arms and tucked her close to his chest.

"Vince, your leg," she protested, but he just chuckled.

"You think I'm going to hurt myself carrying a tiny little thing like you? I don't think so."

He really didn't appear to be having any problems navigating the snow, even on the stairs, and even in dress shoes. He'd grown up in these mountains, and it showed in every confident step he took. He was like a mountain goat, and she felt safe and secure in his strong arms.

Nate met them at the door, holding it open so Vince could stride through. Heat rose to Melanie's face at the way Nate gawked at them; even more so when Vince didn't immediately release her to the ground.

"Vince, let me go," she hissed into his ear.

He gazed down at her and grinned before loosening his hold enough for her to gain her footing.

"I held the fort down for you, bro," Nate assured Vince, jamming his fingers into the pockets of his jeans and rocking back on his heels, a grin firmly secured on his face.

Vince's brow rose. Clearly he wasn't sold.

"You do have a few messages, though," Nate continued. "I've left them for you in your office."

"Okay," he told Nate, and then put a hand on Melanie's shoulder. "I'll walk you to your room first."

"Not necessary. You go do what you need to do. I think I'll just sit out here by the fire for a little while and warm up a bit." She pointed to a plump armchair next to the fireplace, and then rubbed her arms as if still chilled, which, in fact she was, for emphasis.

Vince nodded crisply. "If you'll excuse me, then."

As soon as Vince stepped into the back office, Nate's smile dropped into a worried frown and worry lines appeared over the bridge of his nose. Grabbing Melanie by the elbow, he quickly ushered her into the dining room and out of Vince's earshot.

Jessica, scissors in hand, was just finishing the lace surrounding the candles on the table centerpieces. Baby Gracie had used a nearby chair to pull herself up to a standing position and was "helping" with the decorations, waving strands of multicolored lace ribbons in the air.

As soon as Jessica saw Nate and Melanie enter, she immediately dropped what she was doing, scooped up a protesting Gracie, who didn't want to end her fun with the lace, and moved to confer with them.

"We've got trouble," Nate said in a low voice, without any sort of preamble. The distress written on both her friends' faces was disconcerting.

"What's up?" Melanie asked, discouragement

washing over her. There were any number of possibilities for failure, and she'd probably thought of most of them herself.

"Is it the snowstorm? Did some of the guests not arrive safely?" she asked, listing the two fears highest on her list of worries.

"It's definitely the snowstorm, all right. Our guests have all arrived safely. It's just that—"

"We can't feed them," Jessica interjected. "The catering company we hired backed out on us at the last minute due to the winter storm warning."

"It's plenty treacherous out there, so I get what they're saying. But still, you'd think a catering company in Colorado would be ready for a snowstorm."

"Just not a mountain snowstorm," Jessica said with a soft sigh. "We're really in trouble here, aren't we?"

Melanie was beginning to feel as panicked as Nate and Jessica looked. They'd all put too much time and effort into this fundraiser to let it fail now.

"Have you tried contacting any other caterers? Maybe someone local?" She was certain that would have been the first thing Nate had done, and it was a long shot at best anyway, but she had to ask.

"I called everyone in the phone book," Nate confirmed. "No one is able to fill in last-minute like this. Especially not for as big a function as we're holding."

It had been a roller coaster of a day all around, and Melanie's emotions were in knots, but a new wave of adrenaline kicked in when she realized all their plans were about to come crashing down around them.

"Is the chef here today?" she queried.

"Yes. We've already called him in, along with most of the kitchen staff," Jessica explained. "The problem is, we're not sure what to do with them. On Friday nights, we usually serve meat-loaf and mashed potatoes. That's hardly the sort of thing to serve at a fancy fundraiser."

"Getting all dressed up for *meatloaf?*" Nate screwed up his face in distaste, reminding Melanie of a little boy. She knew Vince and Nate were only two years apart in age, but it sure seemed like more, especially at times like this.

His antics had worked, though, at least for a moment, and both Melanie and Jessica cracked tiny smiles, however short-lived they ended up being.

"Nate's dislike for meatloaf aside," Jessica continued, "we've got a huge problem here."

"Maybe." Melanie scrunched her brow and tapped her chin. "And maybe not."

"What are you thinking?" Nate asked eagerly, clearly relieved that Melanie had *some* suggestion, where he and Jessica had come up blank.

"Is the kitchen well-stocked?" she asked.

"Sure. And we keep a whole large pantry for backup in case of an emergency."

"This is definitely an emergency," Melanie assured him.

"What are we going to do?" Nate's voice bounded around her like a puppy. She hadn't even told him what her plan was and he was already behind it.

She smiled. "We're going to feed our guests a country buffet. Morningway is a rustic lodge. We'll simply serve our guests up a rustic fare."

"Brilliant!" Jessica breathed.

Nate and Jessica passed a look between them at Melanie's accidental use of the word *our*, and she colored.

"I—I want this to go well, especially because I'm finished with my project and it's officially my last night here," she stammered.

Or ever again, for that matter. Although Vince hadn't actually said goodbye when they were dancing at the restaurant, Melanie knew that's what his kiss meant.

Wasn't it?

But she couldn't think about that right now. She had a fundraiser to save. She'd have plenty of time to think—and cry—all she wanted, once she was back in her condo in Boulder.

Alone.

"Jessica, let's you and I go to the kitchen and get things in order there," Melanie said, pulling her mind back into gear. Mentally solving a problem and then physically getting the job done was just what she was used to. And good at.

"We do have one more problem, though," she continued. "And it's a big one."

Nate frowned. "What's that?"

"You're going to have to keep Vince out of the way until we sort all of this out. We not only have to get the dinner going, but we have to get all our guests situated here in the dining room. That's not going to be easy with Vince roaming through the lodge."

Nate squared his shoulders and winked at her. "I'm on it. We've got a generator in the basement that's been giving us problems. I'll take Vince down there. It ought to keep him busy for at least an hour or two."

"All right, then," Melanie said, half feeling like they ought to huddle up like a football squad, star up their hands, and do a group cheer. "Let's do this."

Vince was up to his elbows in grease, he thought, as he crouched on his hands and knees next to the backup generator. Not the best thing to be doing for a guy who was wearing a brand-new white dress shirt.

Or at least, it used to be white.

At least Nate was more appropriately dressed for the job, in his blue jeans and olive-green T-shirt. That said, Nate seemed like he was hanging back and letting Vince do all the work.

Big surprise there.

Nate crouched by his side, cocking his head as if to inspect what he was doing, but Vince knew it was all for show. Nate barely had any grease on him at all.

"Melanie looks nice today," Nate commented, sounding almost *too* casual.

Vince was surprised by the flicker of jealousy that flared in his chest, that another man—his *brother*—found Melanie attractive in any way. Which was, of course, thoroughly ridiculous and unreasonable on any number of levels.

No two ways about it, Melanie was an attractive woman. If a man—any man—looked at her and thought otherwise he was either nuts or blind. And as for Nate, well, he was head over heels in love with Jessica. His off-the-cuff comment had been just that—a comment.

Oh, boy, Vince thought. If he was getting jealous over Nate's meaningless remarks, then he had it *bad*.

"Yeah," he agreed after a pregnant pause. "She is beautiful."

Nate switched his eyes from the generator to Vince, so Vince concentrated his gaze even harder on the tricky old generator. He didn't want Nate to see anything suspect in his eyes, and he wasn't quite sure he could hide what he was feeling inside from his own brother.

"Although," Nate continued, "she does look a

little out of place out here at the lodge. At least today she does, what with wearing those high heels and all."

"Hand me a wrench." Vince scowled. It wasn't something he hadn't thought of a hundred times over the past day, and it sure didn't help to have Nate reiterate what he already knew.

"I don't know, though. She kinda got used to wearing jeans and hiking boots while she was here, don't you think?"

"The wrench?" Vince prompted again. Couldn't his brother just shut up and mind his own business for once?

Nate's gaze hardly wavered from Vince as he reached into the toolbox and handed Vince the wrench he'd requested.

Repeatedly.

"I'd be curious to know how much of this has rubbed off on her. Morningway Lodge, I mean. Do you think she'll keep a little bit of the mountain with her?"

His frown deepening, Vince leaned back on his heels and braced his hands on his thighs. "Hardly likely. I've seen her in her element, and it's not Morningway Lodge. She's much more at home at her office in Boulder, what with the makeup and hair and heels and stuff.

"That's her world. And she's going back there tomorrow. Permanently. So can we please just not talk about it?"

Nate shrugged and flashed his usual carefree grin, that annoying younger-brother smile that Vince often just wanted to punch right off his face. But it wasn't Nate's fault that Vince was in a bad mood; and Nate was Nate after all. Vince knew it was about time he got used to that fact, if he and Nate were going to be working together.

He'd vowed to himself, and God, that he would do better with his brother. Try harder. And there was no time like the present to make good on that promise.

The room was quiet for a moment while both men turned their attention to the backup generator. Nate even got his hands dirty.

Vince was just glad that he could be alone with his thoughts for a moment.

Things had gotten completely out of hand here. Melanie had indicated she had one more detail she needed to cover at the lodge, and then she'd be gone. How long would that take? What if she'd left already?

He wanted to leave and go find her—right now. But he could hardly go and do his own thing with the generator half-finished and people who depended on him. No backup generator available at the lodge in the middle of a blizzard?

Not good.

He sighed and pushed his glasses up the bridge of his nose with the back of his fisted hand.

First the generator. Then Melanie.

He'd just returned his focus to the machine when Nate suddenly climbed to his feet, crossing his arms and staring down at Vince with a funny look in his eyes.

"Do you have feelings for Melanie?" Nate asked, his voice unusually crisp and serious.

Nate's words jolted Vince from his thoughts just as much as his sudden actions had. Vince stood just as abruptly, and almost lost his balance. He would have pitched forward had he not quickly braced himself against the generator.

He'd nearly forgotten that he'd just got his leg out of a cast. Sharp edges of pain shot down his leg and into his foot.

Great. Just what he needed.

"I asked how you feel about her." Nate shifted

his weight and arched one eyebrow, looking for all the world like a wise old owl who already knew the answer to his question.

Like Vince was going to tell *him*.

Not going to happen. Not in this lifetime.

"I don't know what you mean." He clenched his jaw, choosing to focus on his physical pain rather than the intense, throbbing ache in his heart.

Nate snorted. "Right, Vince. Play dumb. Jess and I know what's really going on, so you might as well fess up and admit it."

Vince swiped his hand down the front of his shirt, and then realized he'd created a thick line of grease over the white fabric. He brushed the stain with the back of his hand, but that only made it worse.

Oh, well. It was just a stupid shirt, which at this point, he'd end up throwing in the trash anyway. What was a little more grease in the big scheme of things?

"You're going to stand there and deny everything?" It was a taunt, but there was another subtle level to the question. Nate was being serious for once in his life.

"She's leaving," Vince said defensively. "Tonight. Or maybe tomorrow morning at the latest. Either way, she's out of here, and I doubt she'll even think about me once she's gone. She's got the promotion to director of operations in the bag. I'm happy for her." He hoped he *sounded* happy for her, but he couldn't be sure.

"Yeah, I heard about that." Nate nodded triumphantly, as if he'd just won the game, whatever that was. "Exactly my point."

"Needle-nosed pliers and a flat screwdriver," Vince said aloud, turning to dig through the toolbox. It unnerved him that Nate continued to stare at him like some sort of oddity.

"This isn't something you can fix with tools."

"I've fixed the generator dozens of times." He was exaggerating, and he was purposefully misunderstanding Nate's words.

And they both knew it.

"Hey," said Nate, clasping a firm hand on Vince's shoulder. "I know I'm your little brother and all, and I know you don't really respect my opinion, but this is one instance where I've already been there, bro. I almost waited too long to tell Jessica I was in love with her. It took nearly losing her in the fire at the day care for me to wake up."

Vince just stared at Nate and swallowed hard against the burning in his throat.

"All I'm saying is, don't make the same mistake I did. Don't wait until she's moved on to figure out how you feel about her."

Vince sighed deeply. "I *know* how I feel about her."

"Then tell her."

He couldn't believe he was getting into this with his brother of all people. His business was his business, especially in his personal life. But the compassion, genuine concern and empathy in Nate's expression couldn't be denied, and Vince really did need to talk to someone.

Suddenly, with Nate, there was no teasing. No judgment. He sensed it was a totally different ball game now. Nate was talking to him man to man, not just brother to brother. And he cared.

Vince shook his head. "I wish it were that easy. Every circumstance seems to be working against me, and it turns out that I'm my own worst enemy.

"When I had her alone, I stumbled around trying to find the right words, and then I ended up saying nothing, like the fool that I am. The truth is, I'm afraid to tell her I love her because

I don't know if she feels the same way about me. I'm ashamed to say she's definitely seen me at my worst. More than once."

"All the more reason for her to want to fix you," Nate teased. "Women are like that, you know."

Vince chuckled at his brother's attempt to lighten the mood, but his heart still felt heavy.

"The thing is, I blew it. Missed my opportunity. Now I don't know when I'll get to talk to her before she leaves."

Nate cocked his head to one side and stared at Vince for a long moment. Finally, he smiled. "I know this is going to come as a shock to you, bro, but just leave it to me. This time around, the cup is half-full."

Vince frowned and stared back at Nate. Whatever *that* was supposed to mean.

"I'll take care of the logistics, and you just worry about what you're going to say to her, you dumb ape," Nate said with a shake of his head. "Man, you can really be obtuse sometimes."

Vince opened his mouth to disagree, and then closed it again. Nate was right. He *could* be obtuse. Especially where a certain redhead was concerned.

Chapter Sixteen

For better or for worse, the party was as ready as it was going to be. The decorations were up, the food was cooked, the sound system had been checked and the guests were all seated in place inside the dining room, awaiting the start of the fundraiser.

All that was missing was Vince.

Nate had made good his promise and had kept Vince occupied with the generator. At least that one thing had gone in their favor.

Melanie shifted from foot to foot, waiting. Jessica had just gone down to the basement to see what was keeping them—or rather, covertly, to let Nate know it was time for the fundraiser to start, without tipping Vince off to any of it.

Melanie had never been so nervous in her

life. Her heart was pounding so hard that it was making her head ache. In all her years on the job, and even in her personal life, she had never been as invested in a project as she was now.

If she were being honest with herself, it wasn't so much the project she was invested in as it was the person. When had she fallen so deeply in love with Vince? Now she couldn't even imagine feeling any other way.

She'd done all she could do. Nate and Jessica had done the same. Now it was time for her to put her newfound faith into action and trust God that everything would turn out according to His will.

She was still struggling with the concept of relying on God, although she now knew it in her heart that beyond doubt, her faith was real. Still, it was hard to put her anxiety into His hands.

Please, God, she prayed silently. *Don't let this be a mistake.*

She prayed for Nate's sake, if not for her own.

But especially, she prayed for Vince.

She was nervously pacing and waiting at the top of the stairwell when the three of them returned. Jessica was the first one up. Her eyes widened when she met Melanie's gaze and she mouthed the words, *"Oh, dear!"*

Nate was next, wiping his greasy hands off on a shop rag. He just grinned and shrugged.

And then Vince appeared.

Somewhere along the way he had completely discarded his tie. He was wearing his brand-new crisp white shirt completely untucked, which was not like him at all—at least under normal circumstances.

Worse, the shirt was now covered with streaks of grease. There was even a smudge of grease on his forehead, which Melanie thought was probably a result of his trying to push his glasses up the bridge of his nose.

When he saw Melanie, he nodded at her and brushed at the front of his shirt, which only exacerbated the problem.

"We got the generator working," he informed her, one side of his mouth tipping up into a half grin. "But I'm thinking this shirt might not be salvageable."

Melanie's mouth moved, but no words came out. Still in shock, she had no idea what to say.

"Oh, well," he said with an easy shrug.

Oh, well? Easy for him to say.

Melanie whispered a prayer for patience. Couldn't they get through this evening without yet another catastrophe?

Nate and Jessica weren't dressed up, but that was not without a great deal of foresight. The three of them had decided it would be a dead giveaway if they wore anything fancy; particularly because Nate's idea of dressing up was wearing his U.S. Marine Corps dress blue uniform.

But they had all gone to a great deal of trouble to make sure—in the most underhanded way possible—that *Vince* would be dressed appropriately for the evening to make him feel more comfortable with his image as he walked into the fundraiser.

In hindsight, Melanie decided Nate should definitely have chosen another project with which to distract Vince. Preferably one with less grease.

What in the world were they supposed to do now?

If they asked him to change into another dress shirt, never mind forcing a tie back on him, he would know something was up for sure. Granted, it wouldn't be long before this gig was up anyway, but Melanie didn't want to take the pleasure of surprising him away from the guests who had given so much of themselves just to be here for him tonight.

Short of ushering him into the dining room with grease up to his ears, their only other option was to let him change into whatever he wanted, and then somehow create a valid scenario for getting him into the dining room at all, particularly accompanied by all of them.

Nate, who was the only one out of the line of Vince's sight, met her gaze, twisted his lips to one side and shook his head briefly.

Melanie slid her gaze from Nate to Jessica, silently asking her what they thought she should do. A little help right now would be greatly appreciated.

When no one offered anything, she reached up on tiptoe and brushed the smudge of grease off Vince's forehead with the pad of her thumb.

"You have grease on your face," she told him, her palm brushing across the scratchy surface of his five-o'clock shadow. He was meticulous about shaving, but there was no way she could think of to encourage him to shave without giving everything away.

Nope. Not a chance.

Besides, she liked him a little scruffy, and if they were going to do this thing rustic-style— as it now appeared they would be, given the one-hundred-and-eighty-degree change in the menu and the dress code—a little bit of beard wasn't going to make any difference.

"I really need to wash up and change," Vince commented, as if reading everyone's mind. He held his hands away from his body in an obvious attempt not to spread the grease any further than it already was.

"You know what?" Nate said casually, out of nowhere. "I'm hungry."

"Me, too," Melanie immediately chimed in, although the statement was so far from the truth that it wasn't even funny. She ignored the pointed look Vince flashed at her and the way his eyebrows arched over the top rim of his glasses.

No doubt Vince was aware of how stuffed she was from the lunch they'd had. She'd managed to drag the whole ordeal out for over two hours by eating—*very slowly*—every bite of every course.

But she could see where Nate was going with this, so she could hardly admit she never wanted to see food again as long as she lived— or at least until tomorrow.

"You know what we ought to do?" Jessica suggested, as if the thought had just now occurred to her. "Why don't the four of us have dinner together? Gracie is with her grandfather right now, and believe me, he has more than enough help from the, uh, hospitality staff. Nate and I would love to sit down and have a quiet dinner with you guys, and have some adult conversation for a change. Don't you think that would be glorious?"

Melanie thought Jessica was overselling it by a mile, and that Vince would catch on right away, but he didn't *look* like he suspected anything.

He could have easily bowed out, saying that he was still full from the enormous lunch they'd shared. That wouldn't be a big stretch.

At the very least, Melanie expected him to come up with some flimsy reason or another as to why he could not join them—like that he didn't think Nate was capable of carrying on an *adult* conversation.

Actually, thought Melanie wryly, forget the fine line of courtesy where the two *boys* were concerned. Vince was definitely capable of saying something like that to his brother out loud—right in Nate's face, for that matter.

She couldn't have been more surprised when he nodded in agreement, but Nate and Jessica didn't look as nearly as stunned as she felt.

"Sure, I'd like that. Melanie, do you think you could postpone taking off for Boulder, at least until after dinner?" His blue-eyed gaze met hers and held, an earnest, beseeching look in his eyes.

Melanie was a little shaken up by the odd turn of events, but however it had happened, it was working in their favor. She breathed a heartfelt sigh of relief. "Sure thing. It sounds nice."

And it did.

Even if everything was going to change the moment he walked into the dining room. Even if she was going to try to find a way to slip out of the fundraiser before Vince noticed she was gone—before he had the opportunity to express his anger at her for her duplicity, and for once again taking his brother's side of things.

Even if leaving was going to break her heart.

Vince ran a comb over his unruly dark brown hair, trying to get the front, silver-streaked lock of hair to lie down. Thankfully, lots of guys wore their hair spiked because he couldn't get his hair to do anything else, not even to save his life.

Generally, he was a wash-and-wear kind of guy—not someone who would primp and preen in front of the mirror, like he was doing now. But this was important—maybe the most important night of his life—and he wanted to look his best.

For Melanie.

This was it. Thankfully, his brother and Jessica had thoughtfully given him one more opportunity to speak to Melanie about what was in his heart.

But this was it. Ground zero. Last Chance, Colorado.

For once in his life, he was glad for his brother's interference. If Nate and Jessica had truly had the opportunity for a night to themselves, giving Nate a break from twenty-four-hour-a-day baby duty, they sure wouldn't want to ruin it by spending their time with him and Melanie.

Vince highly suspected that Nate had generously abandoned the idea of a romantic dinner for two—or at least as romantic as one could get at the lodge—to help him get a moment alone with Melanie.

Maybe Nate *did* care.

Vince took one look at his black jeans and maroon western shirt and shrugged at his own reflection. His clothes weren't dressy, but they didn't need to be. Not here at the lodge.

Anyway, how he looked wasn't really going to change a thing, so there was no use shuffling about in his room. It all boiled down to his being able to verbally communicate his feelings to Melanie. And fast.

Locking the door to his room behind him, he hurried down the hallway to where Melanie was waiting. She had a tight smile on her face that made her nose scrunch up in the most adorable way, making her freckles dance. The apprehension in her beautiful copper eyes softened as their gazes met.

"The chef's got good food cooking, and our table is all set," she informed him. "Nate and Jessica are waiting in the dining room for us. This should be fun."

"Sounds good," he replied, running his hand across the back of Melanie's shoulders. She felt tense, so he moved behind her and gently massaged her shoulders.

"Ready to eat again, sweetheart?" he murmured into her ear.

"No, not really," she said with a laugh. She leaned back and smiled at him, and his heart flipped right over. No question about it—his happiness depended on her smiling at him, *frequently,* every single day for the rest of his life.

Their lives.

He couldn't even let himself think of the alternative. He took her hand as she started forward and laced their fingers together, thanking God once again for the reprieve that would allow him to speak to her. But right this second, he was just happy to be with her.

Melanie reached the dining room doors first and paused to look back as her hand met the doorknob, an unreadable expression on her face.

That the dining room doors were closed was peculiar in itself; usually during dinner hours the doors were kept open so guests could dine at their leisure. Vince suddenly experienced a spine-tingling, hair-raising premonition that something wasn't exactly as it should be.

He didn't have time to think what that might be.

Melanie pulled open the doors with a great flourish. Behind those doors, Vince was met with a full room of people, most of whom were familiar to him. Nate and Jessica were there, along with Pop, holding a crowing baby Gracie on his lap. As Melanie urged him to enter, all the guests stood and clapped in his direction.

There must have been a hundred people present, and not one of them were current guests at the lodge—although, he realized as he looked around the room in a dazed shock, many of these people had been residents at the lodge at one time or another.

Nate and Jessica, and even Melanie, had turned toward him and were applauding with the crowd.

What *was* this? And why were they all applauding *him?*

He turned around, ready to exit the room— at least until he'd had the chance to regroup and figure out what was going on—but Melanie blocked his way and nodded toward the small stage where worship bands sometimes played. Nate had already ascended the platform and was reaching for the microphone. Vince only now realized that in addition to the well-dressed guests and the fancy decorations, the sound system had been set up.

"Come on up here, Vince," Nate said, gesturing to his right side.

Vince took another stunned look around the room. All eyes were on him, as if they expected—what?

He hadn't a clue. But it didn't take a genius to realize he'd been set up. Nate was obviously the chief instigator of this shenanigan, but clearly Jessica—and more surprisingly, Melanie—had been in on it.

He'd thought Melanie knew him better than that. He hated big crowds, especially if the attention was centered directly upon him. And for some reason, that's exactly what she done to him. But why?

He'd never felt so uncomfortable in his life. All of the guests were fashionably garbed—the ladies in pretty dresses and the men in suits and ties. No wonder Melanie had insisted on his fancy get-up this morning.

"Vince?" Nate prompted, with that annoying, nutty-younger-brother grin of his splitting his face.

It was clear there was no way out of this

predicament except to go through with it. So Vince squared his shoulders, lifted his chin and marched toward the stage—but not before flashing Melanie a pointed glare, mentally posing the question he could not yet ask aloud, and letting her know there would be no question that he was going to ask her later.

Why'd you do this to me?

Her answering expression was grim.

"Most everyone here is acquainted with Vince, and you know how important his work is here at Morningway Lodge. Many of you have been touched by his warmth and kindness over the years. This ministry would be nonexistent if it weren't for him. Let's give him another round of applause as he makes his way to the stage."

Vince stepped up on the platform, held out his hands and shook his head, wishing this would all go away. But that didn't stop everyone in the room from their misguided but well-meant applause.

He didn't like it, but he appreciated it. It must be some truly momentous occasion for all these people to have gathered together, particularly in view of the snowstorm.

Nate, on the other hand, had just been officially bumped up to the top of Vince's hit list. Not that he hadn't already been there before, but now his name was in bold, capitalized red lettering with several asterisks beside it.

"As you all know," Nate continued, "our day care recently burned down, a facility that many of you and your children used on your visit here. It's a critical aspect of this ministry and needs to be rebuilt as soon as possible to accommodate all of our guests' small children. But rebuilding takes a considerable amount of money, funding that, quite frankly, we simply don't have."

Vince cringed, and it was all he could do not to clench his fists and give away what he was really thinking. His heart was hammering and his mind was flitting from fact to fact with no real cohesion.

Morningway Lodge was a ministry more than it was a business. Fundraisers were typically a given in such work, and certainly his father had hosted his fair share.

Vince, however, hadn't followed in his father's footsteps. He was determined to make it on his own. For him, it was humiliating to even think about asking people for a handout, even if it was with kind, good-hearted people and for a good cause. Nate had just shared the most intimate details of their family business for everyone to hear. All of the stuff Vince *never* talked about—the heavy, dark burden he chose rather to bear upon his own shoulders.

His stomach churned slowly and he wasn't sure how much longer he'd be able to fight the queasy feeling. And if that wasn't bad enough, he thought his bad leg might just give out on him. He was more than a little grateful when Melanie turned up next to him and put an arm around his waist.

Not so much, when she took the microphone from Nate and started speaking to the crowd.

"I've had the privilege of working alongside this man for the past six weeks," she began, her voice raising in pitch and enthusiasm with every word. Vince wanted to cringe. The strained smile on his face was beginning to ache.

Here it came, and he wasn't ready for it. She was either going to tease him mercilessly about his poor organizational skills, bringing them to light in front of this crowd, or else she would have to say something inane—and probably untrue—about him. Either way, it wouldn't be good.

"I was hired to change Vince's business around. Instead, my time with Vince has changed me. I've watched him work quietly in the background, ministering to others and asking for nothing in return, especially any sort of recognition or accolades.

"As you already know, that's why we're all here tonight, to recognize him and his work. We're here to show our appreciation for all he has done here at Morningway Lodge. Vince has given so much of himself for all of us. What do you say we direct some of that love back to him?"

The crowd cheered heartily in response.

"I ask that you give as God would lead you, out of the generosity of your hearts, so that the day care can be built and reopened for the precious children as soon as possible. God bless you."

As Melanie handed the microphone back to Nate, the guests' cheering turned into a loud, happy roar. Vince stood frozen to the spot, struggling between the warmth of self-consciousness flushing into his face and, despite everything, the love and appreciation for Melanie ballooning in his chest.

How could he not be moved?

They had gone to all this trouble for him and for the lodge? He could hardly wrap his mind around what was happening. All these people were willing to dig sacrificially into their own pockets to get the day care rebuilt— just because someone asked them to.

Tears of appreciation stung in his eyes. He would normally have been mortified by such an emotion shown publicly, but not now. He didn't think he'd ever been more grateful than he was at this moment, and it was all due to the wonderful people in this room. He didn't know how to express what he was feeling, to let everyone know how much it meant to him that they truly cared.

Pop was sitting on his wheelchair with Gracie on his lap, beaming proudly at Vince from across the room. He'd worked his whole life to see that look.

Jessica was standing directly behind his father, one hand on his shoulder. When their eyes met, she gave him a big smile and a thumbs-up.

Nate placed the microphone down and placed his hands together prayer-style, offering one last silent thank you to his big brother.

Melanie simply held one hand over her heart and cried. Her sweet, glistening tears changed his whole world.

If only she knew.

Chapter Seventeen

The fundraiser was over. The guests were dispersing. An incredible amount of money had been donated by the generous patrons—enough to cover the cost of rebuilding the day care and then some.

Earlier, Melanie had slipped into the kitchen, thinking it would be the best place for a safe getaway, while still being able to hear what was happening in the dining room. There was plenty to be done, and not nearly enough help, especially when the dirty plates started piling up, so she donned an apron and set her mind to washing dishes; but her heart was in the other room, with Vince.

There were still many more dishes to do, and the kitchen was still clamoring with lodge employees going in and out the door, but

Melanie knew she couldn't wait much longer to depart the premises.

Not if she was going to make a clean getaway.

Melanie wanted to leave. She *should* leave. She knew it would be best for everyone if she just got out of the way—permanently. But there seemed to be some intangible force holding her back. Her curiosity was getting the best of her, and she couldn't help but want to know the end of the story.

Not wanting to be noticed, she hovered just inside the kitchen door to see how things played out.

Nate was pacing back and forth in the dining room, his hands clasped behind his back. His thoughts were apparently going the same direction as hers. It wouldn't be long now.

Vince was saying goodbye to the last of the guests, but she and Nate both knew he would return. There was some kind of confrontation brewing this evening, no matter which way the pendulum swung.

And that was just it, she supposed. The only reason she'd stayed as long as she had, she told herself, was that she wanted to see for herself if Vince and Nate were finally going to be able to be reconciled together.

Well, that, and the fact that the dishes weren't yet finished. She could help with that at least, before she left the lodge for good. It went completely against the grain for her to leave a project half-finished, and she wouldn't start now.

Not with the dishes, and not with the brothers.

She couldn't just walk away without some sort of closure, without ever knowing for sure what happened—with Vince and Nate, that is, and not with what she felt for Vince. The conclusion to their story had been sealed with a kiss at lunchtime.

A goodbye kiss.

Nibbling nervously on her lower lip, she stayed in the shadows, crossed her fingers and prayed for the best—because she well knew that the exact opposite of their best intentions could very well happen.

Vince could be furious with Nate.

And with her.

All the more reason she should leave now, while the going was good.

At this point she put the odds at about fifty-fifty as to which way it would go. She knew

Vince well enough to see how uncomfortable he'd been up there on the stage. And despite the fact that they'd done so well with the fundraiser, there was still the fact that everyone Vince trusted had gone behind his back, raising funds with a method that Vince, had he known about it in advance, would have rejected outright.

She pulled herself even deeper into the shadows when Vince stomped back into the room, a livid, palpable energy upon him that Melanie had never seen before. His dark stare covered the room from one side to the other. He was obviously looking for someone.

Maybe her. Her breath caught and held. The odds were getting worse by the second because Vince's expression gave away exactly what he was thinking.

He was furious. And, in Melanie's absence, he was headed straight for Nate. Like a scene in a B-rated horror flick, Melanie couldn't seem to tear her gaze away, even though she'd suddenly decided she didn't really want to see what happened next.

Vince stopped before Nate and grabbed the front of his shirt in his fist, pulling Nate forward until they were face to face. Melanie didn't know whether it was good or bad that she could see every little detail that was going on from her hiding place behind the kitchen door. This looked like it was going to be a real humdinger of a fight, worse than anything she had seen between the brothers in the past.

Nate stood his ground, his expression still full of that boyish charm that Melanie well knew—as Nate knew—would silently provoke Vince to do his worst, despite the fact that Vince held him tight with one fist while the other was thrust upward just underneath his chin.

"Nate, you've done some mighty stupid things in your life," Vince hissed through his teeth, nearly lifting Nate off his feet.

Melanie held her breath. Nate still didn't appear all that concerned about the situation, even though he'd leaned forward and was eye to eye with Vince.

It occurred to her that *she* might be more concerned about the situation than either one of them. The two men were puffing up against each other like a couple of roosters. Guys could be so stubborn that way, nearly forgetting what they were even fighting about in their quest to be the victor.

The two brothers were the same height,

and while they were close in physical build, Melanie thought Nate might have the advantage, which was maybe why his goofy grin remained. From his time in the Marines, Nate was somewhat broader than Vince, making him appear slightly bigger, although Vince definitely looked more menacing.

They were pretty evenly matched, but there was always the possibility that Nate would best Vince in a fight.

Unless she had Vince's back. Fair fight or not, Melanie didn't want Vince to get hurt. What a horrible end to the night that would be.

She tensed, ready to spring forward, before she realized how ridiculous she was being. What was she going to do, pounce on them both and knock their heads together? It would have been laughable, if it wasn't so serious.

The moment dragged on for a lifetime.

"Mighty stupid things," Vince repeated with a growl. "But this—what happened tonight—" he paused for several seconds before continuing "—*isn't* one of them. Man, you knew I wouldn't go for a public fundraiser, but you did it anyway. You're crazy, you know that?"

Laughing heartily, he clapped his arms

around Nate and picked him off the floor in a giant hug. Nate crowed and pulled back at him and after a moment it looked like the two men were wrestling with one another rather than hugging it out.

Men!

Melanie's sigh of relief was so large that she nearly sank to the floor from it. Tears flowing from her eyes, Melanie's grip tightened on the door. Her whole heart and soul was with those men and what was happening out there in the middle of the dining room. She wanted to run out and throw herself right into the middle of that big bear hug.

But that couldn't happen. She just didn't think her heart could handle it. She knew perfectly well that she was the world's biggest chicken. She could hear herself clucking inside her head.

And yet she wasn't moving.

"I'm sorry for the way I've treated you." Melanie wasn't surprised that Vince was the first to speak.

"Apology accepted," Nate answered, nodding as if that were his due. He waited until everyone's surprised gazes were on him before grinning. "And I'm sorry I left you in the lurch."

Vince clapped Nate on the shoulder, matching him grin for grin. "Apology accepted."

Jessica, carrying baby Gracie, moved to Nate's side, looking as relieved as Melanie felt. Vince and Nate's father wheeled up behind them, his expression pleased and proud. It was a good day for the Morningways.

But she was not a Morningway, and it was time for her to go.

"You know how hard it is for me to say the words," Vince said, clapping Nate on the back. His chest was full of so many raw emotions that he thought it might burst. "But thank you. Believe me when I say that I truly thank God that I have such a stubborn brother."

Nate grinned. "I'd hoped you'd feel that way. I have to say, I was planning on running the other direction if you came down hard on me."

Jessica chuckled and ran a hand over Nate's forearm. "Sure you were. The way I saw it, you were about to jump down Vince's throat. The whole family saw you two starting to square off, so don't even try to say otherwise."

"I'll be a witness to that," Pop said. "You boys always were roughhousing each other."

"Uh-oh," added Gracie definitively.

Everyone laughed at the baby's apt words.

"Speaking of family," Vince said, his brow knit, "has anyone seen Melanie? The guests swamped me during the fundraiser. I don't think I've seen her around since after she left the stage area."

"Melanie? Family?" Pop teased, a delighted smile on his face. "What have I missed here? I have the feeling it's something important."

"Yeah," Vince agreed, his heart swelling. "It is important. But I'll explain it all to you later. Right now I've got to find her."

"Go get her," Jessica urged. Gracie bounced excitedly, babbling and waving her arms in wild abandon.

"It appears Gracie agrees with you," Pop commented with a grin.

"Go, man, go," Nate pressed, turning his brother around by the shoulders. "She can't have gotten far."

Vince didn't need urging. He thought his heart might burst if he didn't find her soon. But where to look?

He'd expected she would stick around after

the fundraiser was over, like his family had. Now he had to wonder, had she just up and left?

It looked that way. She obviously wasn't in the dining hall, and he'd been in the front room receiving his guests only minutes before, so she hadn't gotten out that way.

Focus, Vince thought to himself. *Think through this logically. Where would she have gone?*

Back to Boulder probably. That made the most sense.

Back to her room. She'd have to get her stuff together to leave, right?

Unless she was already packed and ready to go, which was always a possibility.

Why hadn't he paid more attention?

His family looked on as Vince struggled to compose his thoughts. He couldn't seem to put anything reasonable together to save his life. He shouldn't be in a panic. At the very worst, she would, indeed, have left for Boulder, and he would follow her and find her.

But this evening had been without a doubt the best night of his life. It was not the money so much, although of course he was totally floored by the incredible way God had moved so that they would be able to rebuild the day care.

The true marvel was in all the people who had come from all over to show their support. His faith had been floundering. He'd often wondered if his ministry meant anything to anyone.

And now he knew it had, and he was grateful.

Truly, this was the best night of his life, bar none, he thought. As if the successful fundraiser hadn't been enough, he was finally, well and truly reconciled with Nate. Things would be different from here on out, surrounded by the support of his family. He just knew it.

With Melanie in his arms to share all these blessings with, the night would be perfect.

Without her, it felt empty somehow.

Nate's voice jolted him back to the moment, if not into action. "What are you doing just standing there like a blooming idiot?"

"Nate!" Jessica exclaimed, elbowing her fiancé in the ribs. "Don't be rude. Vince, why don't you go ask the waitstaff if they happened to see her? I can still hear them banging around in the kitchen."

It was a place to start. Nodding his head to Jessica in gratitude, he practically ran into the kitchen, swinging the door wide and barging in like a raging bull lurching out of the shoot on an eight-second timer.

"Has anyone here seen Melanie Fra—" His words were abruptly cut off as he accidentally barreled right into someone. All he could see was a flurry of red hair and white apron as he instinctively reached to steady her.

Melanie.

Relief flushed through him, followed by a wave of indignant offense. What was she doing skulking around in the kitchen when she should be out celebrating with the family?

"What are you doing back here?" he demanded, trying but failing to soften the edge to his voice. He was so relieved that he wanted to hug her and never let go. Or shake her silly for making him worry that way. "I thought maybe you'd already left."

Melanie stepped completely out of his arms and looked at her feet. "I'd planned to."

Vince gently tipped her beautiful, heart-shaped face up to meet his gaze, and then reached for both of her hands.

"To what?" he murmured, trying to swallow away the burn of emotion in his throat. "Be gone?"

She looked miserable. Deep sorrow had turned her eyes into a compelling, burnished dark copper as she nodded to affirm his question. Her jaw was tight. Her lips were pinched.

She had meant to leave.

Pulling her hands away from his, she yanked on the strings of the apron tied behind her back and turned to hang it on the hook on the wall. She didn't turn back to meet his gaze, but stood staring in the other direction, her arms folded tightly.

"I didn't see the point of sticking around once the fundraiser was in full swing," she explained, her voice scratchy. "But then I got wrapped up in washing dishes, so here I am."

She didn't sound pleased by the prospect.

"I thought you'd stay," Vince said slowly, enunciating his words, "because you worked so hard to put this fundraiser together. You should be celebrating with us, sweetheart, not running away."

"No," she whispered softly. "This is your day. Go spend it with your family."

She wasn't listening to him, or else she was purposefully ignoring what he was saying to her. He tried a new tactic.

"You can't leave yet."

Her eyes widened, but he didn't let her speak.

"We have some things to discuss before you can officially wrap up this project. Why don't we find some place to sit down?"

"I'm sorry—the project? Did I overlook something?" She sounded confused, as well she ought to be. Her *project* had exceeded everyone's expectations by miles and miles. But as he'd said, there was something left to do.

He looked her straight in the eyes. "Yes, ma'am, you did. And we're going to take care of it right now."

She couldn't have looked more stunned than if he'd zapped her with a Taser, but she allowed him to lead her back to the dining hall, which was, thankfully, now empty. His family must have realized what was going on and decided to give them a little privacy.

Reaching for the nearest chair, he seated her and then pulled up a chair for himself sitting opposite her.

By then she seemed to have composed herself and was sitting straight-backed against the edge of her chair, her hands folded in her lap and her expression businesslike and neutral. It hit him like a punch to the gut.

Man, but she was beautiful. And kind. And sensitive. And giving. And…he could go on forever.

Or he could tell her how he felt.

"About the project," he said, resting his forearms on his knees and leaning forward until he'd seized her gaze. "There are a few last-minute details I'd like to clear up."

Her right eyebrow arched up, that cute little twitching thing she did when she was thinking hard. "Like?"

"Well, for one thing, I'd like the name of the CEO of Boulder Business Services because you should get more than just a promotion, though certainly you deserve that. They don't pay you enough for what you do."

She shook her head, still looking a little bemused. "And you know that how?"

"Because whatever salary you're making, it can't possibly compensate for the job you've done here at Morningway Lodge. You've not only straightened out my business, you've also straightened out my life. I'm a better man because of the time we've spent together, and words can't express what I owe you."

A single tear ran down her cheek, and her gaze dropped to her hands on her lap.

"Aw, don't cry." Vince trembled. He didn't know what to do with a woman's tears, especially Melanie's. He hadn't meant to make her cry.

His heart thrumming madly, he reached out and wiped the moisture away with his thumb. She still wouldn't look at him, so he framed her face with his hands and directed her gaze to his. The citrus scent of her hair sent his head awhirl, as if he wasn't already dizzy with emotion.

"You have no idea what it means to hear you say that," she whispered. "I'll always treasure my time at the lodge. With you."

She smiled, lighting up the whole room—or at least to Vince, it seemed that way.

"I've learned so much in the past six weeks," she continued. "I'm completely in awe of the way God worked to provide funding for the day care. It's overwhelming to me even to think about.

"I've seen faith in action—*real* faith, through

you. You don't just talk about Jesus, or throw God around as a weapon. You live, and you love, and you serve. I thank God every day that I met you because if I hadn't taken this one last project, I wouldn't have faith in my life."

Vince was thrilled beyond words at her admission. He'd suspected a spiritual change, but had waited for her to tell him on her own time. But now what she was saying didn't make any sense.

He shook his head adamantly. "I don't know how that can be. I've never wavered in my faith in God the way I've done the past few weeks. I'm ashamed that you had to see it. What you've seen in me is a clear-cut manual on how *not* to live the Christian life."

"That's just it," she said, running a palm over his stubbly cheek. "That's how I could see that your faith was real. It's one thing to believe in God when everything is going right in your life, but it's another to have faith when things go wrong. You wavered but you never doubted. You fought with yourself, not God. God was always there, the one constant that makes your life different from others."

"I don't know what to say," he said, at once bemused and yet as full of joy as he'd ever been. Somehow God had used him to really make a difference in someone's life.

In Melanie's life.

"Yes, I do too know what to say," he amended hastily.

Reaching for both of her hands, he slid to one knee. His bad knee, unfortunately. He was shaky enough as it was. But he didn't care. Not now.

"I love you," he whispered in awe.

Why had he had so much trouble saying those words? If someone had socked him in the chin, he couldn't have been more staggered and surprised. It was so simple, just to say the words. What had he been waiting for?

"I *love* you," he said again, wanting to say the words over and over just because he could. "I panicked when I thought you had left because we had unfinished business. This afternoon at the restaurant, I choked up when I tried to tell you how I felt. I kissed you, but I couldn't seem to be able to speak."

"I thought you were saying goodbye," she said in a hushed tone.

"Never," he vowed. "I don't want you to leave. Not now. Not ever."

He shook his head and pinched his lips into a tight frown. "I wanted to have a ring and make sure everything was perfect when I did this, but now that I'm finally talking, my heart just won't wait. Will you marry me? Will you be my wife?"

"It *is* perfect," she whispered.

"Then you'll marry me?" he asked eagerly. "I'm not moving until you say the words."

"Of course I'll marry you. Now get off your bad knee before you hurt yourself again."

He rose, pulled her into his arms and brushed his lips across hers. As he picked Melanie up and swung her around, he was so happy that he thought he might float right off the ground with her. He wondered if she felt the same way, although technically, her feet really *were* in the air.

"I love you," he said again. It was remarkably easy to say. What an idiot he'd been.

She placed her hands on his shoulders and reached up to kiss his cheek. "I love you, too, with my whole heart, and I can't get over how it happened. I wasn't even looking for love. I'm astounded by God's grace. I've been waiting for you my whole life and I didn't even know it."

His lips hovered over hers, their breath mingling. "Well, you know what they say," he said with a chuckle. "Good things come to those who wait."

* * * * *

Dear Reader:

Can true, happily-ever-after love happen in six weeks? It did for me! While I'm no doubt the exception to the rule, I knew right away that Joe was the one for me. We were engaged practically right away, and were married six months to the day after we met. This month we celebrate our twenty-fourth wedding anniversary, and I love him more than ever.

I hope you've enjoyed reading Vince's story as much as I enjoyed writing it. If you missed Nate's story, which was published in October 2010, I hope you'll look it up—it's still available online. Thank you for coming along for the ride with me through these two stories set at Morningway Lodge.

Nothing makes my day like hearing from my readers. You can email me at DEBWRTR@aol.com, or you can find me on Facebook.

Keep the Faith,

Deb Kastner

QUESTIONS FOR DISCUSSION

1. Vince is a proud man, and stubborn to a fault. He has a hard time asking for and accepting help from others. Do you find yourself hesitant to ask others for help when you need it?

2. Which character in *A Colorado Match* do you most relate to? Why?

3. Melanie's stepfather used the Bible as a weapon. How can she overcome the issues she faces because of that?

4. Vince sometimes could not feel his faith in God, even though he knew in his heart that God was there. What are the dangers in relying on your feelings in your Christian walk?

5. What is the major theme of this novel? How does it relate to where you are at in your Christian walk?

6. God started speaking to Melanie's heart not through Vince's words, but in his actions. How can you witness to others through your actions?

7. Vince and Nate haven't gotten along with each other since the two were children. Why do you think that is? As adults, how can they overcome this issue?

8. Is it important for Vince to forgive Nate for leaving the lodge? Why?

9. Is Morningway Lodge more of a business or a ministry? Can it be both?

10. Vince thought he'd been denied the opportunity to follow his dreams, when actually, he was right where he wanted to be, and where God wanted him. Have you ever been denied a dream? How has God worked through those circumstances?

11. Melanie is coming to a new life in Christ from an anti-Christian background. How

do you think she can learn the things she needs to know to walk in Christ?

12. Morningway Lodge is Jason Morningway's legacy to his sons. How has that affected their lives?

13. Melanie found a way she could help at the hospital by reading books to the children. Do you volunteer in your own community? Why or why not?

14. Melanie was a chronic organizer. She liked to fix things, both physically and emotionally, and struggled when she was not in control of a situation. Can you relate?

15. What is the takeaway value of this book? What will you remember the most?

LARGER-PRINT BOOKS!

GET 2 FREE LARGER-PRINT NOVELS PLUS 2 FREE MYSTERY GIFTS

Love Inspired®

Larger-print novels are now available...

LILP11

SUSPENSE

RIVETING INSPIRATIONAL ROMANCE

Watch for our series of edge-
of-your-seat suspense novels.
These contemporary tales
of intrigue and romance
feature Christian characters
facing challenges to their faith...
and their lives!

**AVAILABLE IN REGULAR
& LARGER-PRINT FORMATS**

For exciting stories that reflect traditional values,
visit:
www.ReaderService.com